I0775435

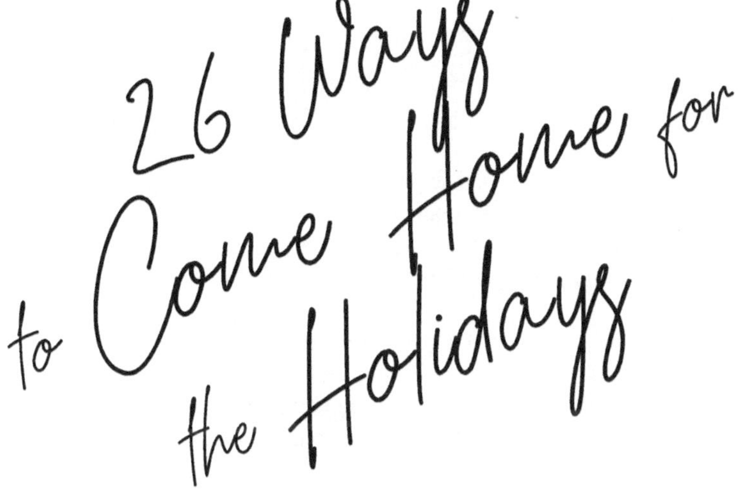

A Thanksgiving-to-Christmas Novella

By Jennifer Joy

FOXBURG & STERN Books, LLC

Editor
Maithy Vu

Proofreader
Babs Grizwald

Copyright © 2023 Foxburg & Stern Books, LLC.
ISBN 979-8-218-21366-4 (paperback)
ISBN 979-8-218-22708-1 (ebook)
Library of Congress Control Number: 2023909817

Visit www.FoxburgAndStern.com for more info.

Cover by MAD Book Covers

*For John and Joyce, who would've been the same ages
as Private Joe and Santa Belle Mina at the time this
book was set.*

"Christmas wouldn't be Christmas without the fun of the Kaufmann's windows. Why, the excitement starts and young heads fill with dreams as soon as the words 'let's go' are heard. And can you remember a Christmastime when there wasn't a special trip to see Kaufmann's windows—that magic moment when Christmas really began?"

-Pittsburgh Post-Gazette, *1941*

THANKSGIVING 1942

Chapter 1

"Stella, that miserable bum has run off—"

"Have you checked the bar? They're not open today, but with him you never know and—"

"No, no! It's for real this time. Trust me. Meet downstairs?"

The exchange Stella just had with Hector over the in-store telephone repeated in her ears as she bolted off the wooden escalator and sped across the first floor of Hanover's Department Store.

She rounded the tea sets in Silverware, flashed a nervous smile at the white-haired salesman stocking gloves in Leather Goods, continued into Books, then—

"Ouch!"

—rammed her thigh straight into the corner of a table. She quickly steadied a stack of *For Whom the Bell Tolls* just in time to keep it from toppling, then rubbed her leg as she hurried on.

Another bruise for the list, she thought, hoping this one hadn't torn her stocking. This was her last decent pair.

She'd expected getting downtown's biggest department store ready for the holidays was going to be a big job, but never guessed how physical it would be. In the past week alone, her pumps had gnawed angry blisters into her heels, she had a bruise on her elbow that she was sure would last until spring, and the red fingernail polish she'd splurged on had already chipped thanks to two weeks' worth of unpacking crates full of Christmas decorations.

Stella skidded out into the aisle and took in her first glimpse of Cosmetics' holiday decor. Garland dripping with crystal-and-gold ornaments that she'd sketched out months ago now crisscrossed the first floor's ceiling. Expensive white goose-feather trees glimmered atop each cosmetics bay (replacements for the fake green German trees everyone was tossing out with the war still on). A handful of salesgirls who'd volunteered for Thanksgiving afternoon shifts buzzed about with armloads of wreaths. She still couldn't quite believe it as she hobbled along— her holiday design sketches had been brought to life.

She should be glowing with pride, but this business with Sal running off...Hector had to be exaggerating, right?

The salesgirls snapped to attention when they saw her.

"Happy Thanksgiving, Miss West," one said.

Stella forced a smile, determined not to show a hint of worry.

"Happy Thanksgiving, ladies. It looks breathtaking so far."

She moved on toward Fine Jewelry, thigh throbbing, when Eleanor stepped out from Handkerchiefs, blocking her path.

"Stella West, always speeding along," Eleanor chided. She wore a green dress speckled with white dots and held a load of him-and-her handkerchief sets against her chest.

"Well—" Stella shrugged with a polite smile, hoping to pass.

Eleanor was the biggest gossip in the store despite the fact that she was old enough to be Stella's grandmother.

"I'm surprised to see you here," Eleanor continued. "Thought for sure you'd be spending Thanksgiving with a beau tonight. Or your father at least. Speaking of, I haven't seen him at Mass for weeks."

"He hurt his leg on the job," Stella said, rubbing her thigh again, thinking of the irony. "He's staying home until it mends, so..."

Eleanor put her hand to her chest. "Oh dear! In a fire?"

"No, no. A tiny accident at the fire station, actually. A twisted knee is all. He doesn't like to talk about it."

Eleanor nodded in exaggerated relief. "Well, still, you should be home with him." She leaned her doughy face closer, whispering, "Or a husband. You young girls all work too much if you ask me." She winked.

I didn't ask, Stella wanted to say, glancing past the old clerk and willing Hector to appear.

"Now, do tell." Eleanor stepped close enough for Stella to smell coffee on her breath. "How are the windows coming? Any hints on a theme this year?"

"Oh, you know that's a secret."

"Well, if this is any indication—" she nodded toward Cosmetics, "—you'll really wow the city this year. We're all depending on you!"

"Mm-hmm." Stella sidestepped her, trying to signal the conversation was over as professionally as she could.

Behind her, Eleanor turned her rambling to the salesgirls.

"My daughter's bringing the whole family down for Saturday's big reveal. Our grandkids are so excited. The littlest one is finally old enough to know all about St. Nicholas and..."

Stella cringed as their excited chatter faded behind her.

Yes, everyone in the city was anticipating the annual unveiling of Hanover's Christmas windows, this year more than ever. Over the summer, Ira Hanover, the store's third-generation owner, had shelled out $10 million of his own money—a literal fortune—to transform the store's twelve-floor downtown location into one that could compete with the big department stores in New York. All the papers had dubbed it "Hanover's Folly"— America had been at war for almost a year now. Sales were down. Families were spending conservatively.

Then, everything changed on re-opening day. A crowd stretching two city blocks waited outside in the August heat to be among the first inside. Men packed into the new Phonographs & Radios department to watch daily demonstrations of the latest models. Women streamed into the Fur Salon for sable stoles, ermine gloves, lynx scarves, and minks. The expanded salon was booked out a full month in advance. The Toy department now filled the entire fifth floor, setting a record as the biggest toy department in town.

The transformation had gone gangbusters, and business never slowed down. Hanover's had become a destination overnight, swiping shoppers from Woolworth to Saks by selling everything from war bonds to top hats. Some new additions followed Ira Hanover's biggest rule: keep customers inside. Four new restaurants now served up coffee, sandwiches, and pie from open until close. Even for those with no money, there was plenty to see. The stockroom on Eleven was now an auditorium where local college students put on free plays and puppet shows, and the store sold nickel bags of peanuts. Some families showed up just to ride the twelve floors of wooden escalators. (The bane of Stella's existence.

She'd broken at least two pairs of pumps since they were installed).

The store's surprise success and increased press attention put even more pressure than ever on this year's Christmas window display—and on Stella, the store's first-ever Head of Holidays.

A hell of a job I'm doing, she thought, *if Hector's right.* She slipped behind the Fine Jewelry counter and pushed through the unmarked stockroom door.

"Hello?" she called, blinking as her eyes adjusted to the dim light, unsure if she'd beat him there or not. She squeezed down the corridor that served as rear access to the twenty-six windows that wrapped around the corner of the store in an L-shape. Boxes towered on either side of her, making her shuffle through sideways in some places.

Her stomach tightened—the silence wiping away any sensation of success she'd felt at the sight of the shimmering first floor. There was no sign of Hector or Sal, but worse, there was no sound of work happening. Opposite Window #6, Sal's makeshift desk (a stack of milk crates because that was all that could fit in the narrow space) was topped with work orders, plans, chewing gum wrappers...and one cold cup of coffee.

The stockroom door flung opened behind her.

"Stella?"

Her heart jumped. "Behind Six!"

Seconds later, Hector Donovan, the store's press agent, was squeezing down the corridor toward her. Hector was a ringer for Cary Grant—tall and always impeccably dressed in a three-piece suit. Today's choice came with a green pocket square. Normally, his wavy black hair was perfectly slicked to the side, a la Grant, except now a few stray locks fell across his forehead. *And* he had his glasses on, which he almost never wore.

All bad signs.

Stella winced. "You're really certain he's not just at the bar again?"

Hector held up a hand. "Forget Sal for a minute. What happened to your dad?"

"My dad? Wait, did Eleanor—?"

Hector nodded.

"Darn her!" Stella put her hands on her hips. "He's fine. He tripped backward over a hose when he was washing the truck at the station."

"Oh." Hector's shoulders relaxed a little. Then he smirked. "Well, now we know where you get your clumsiness from."

She gave him a look. "I'm not clumsy," she said, casually rubbing her thigh again. "And it's not all roses. He tore two muscles around his kneecap. He's healing, but the doctor thinks he should retire. Please don't tell anyone. He's so embarrassed. Eleanor's been digging—"

"Ugh! You bet." Hector pulled a telegram from his pocket. "Well, that leaves us with only *one* crisis on our hands. See here? We've been ditched for a museum in Paris."

"No."

He handed it to her. There it was, in horrible black ink.

```
H. DONOVAN-
URGENT JOB IN PARIS. MUSEUMS BID BIGGER!
UNABLE TO COMPLETE WINDOWS. TELL STELLA
FOR ME. HAPPY HOLIDAYS.
SAL SULLIVAN
```

"Christ on a bike!" Stella swore. Her gaze snapped up to Hector, who was pulling a pack of Lucky Strikes from his pocket. "But Sal has a contract. He's our lead window designer, our *only* designer per his requirement, and he's run off? Why'd he send this to you, not me?"

"You know how he was about…you know…having a woman above him."

She rolled her eyes and reached for the telephone. "Have you tried his apartment? Maybe we can—"

Hector waved her off. "I just hung up with his wife. According to her, his plane's already gone, and he's taken *his mistress* with him. Apparently, he's been running around with her for weeks when he should've been here working. I'm guessing that's what all this is." He pointed his cigarette at the boxes around them.

Stella crumpled the telegram into a ball. "Oh, I knew he was a miserable little weasel, but I thought he was at least *our* weasel, and we'd only have to put up with him for a few more days." She ran her hands down the side of her face. "Ira's going to be furious."

Hector lit his cigarette and combed his hair back. "How close was he to being done?"

"I'm not sure. You know how he is. Or *was*." She snatched up a large silver keyring from Sal's desk.

Because the fifth floor was entirely devoted to toys, Stella had focused all her attention on transforming it into Santa's Village, and at Ira's suggestion, had hired Sal Sullivan away from a huge store in Manhattan to execute her window designs.

She groaned, flipping through the keyring for Window #6. "I never should've agreed to leave him so unsupervised. 'Watchful eyes cramp the creative spirit.' Isn't that how he put it?"

"Should we telephone Ira?" Hector said, puffing nervously.

"And ruin his Thanksgiving?" Stella shook her head, unlocking the miniature door to Window #6. She yanked it open. The curtain that blocked the glass on the street side blotted out all the light inside.

"Lighter?"

Hector handed it over as Stella put a knee up to crawl inside the display. She felt his hand steady her back ever so lightly as she climbed inside.

She flicked it on.

"Oh no. Oh, that loaf!" she gasped, surveying the twenty square feet of unpacked boxes. This year's secret theme, *Home for the Holidays*, was to be a heart-tugger for families, especially for those with loved ones away at war. Different windows were to depict all types of homes celebrating Christmas: a living room piled with toys and gifts, an igloo filled with penguins, elves in Santa's workshop, and even an angel-filled Heaven. Window #6 was supposed to be *Countryside Christmas*, a snowy slope brought to life with animated forest creatures and Santa standing in the middle, waving.

"How bad is it?" Hector called. "Are our gooses cooked?"

"Charbroiled. We need to check the rest!"

Within a span of ten minutes, Stella and Hector had swept through the whole corridor. Out of twenty-six windows, only two appeared to be completely finished. The rest had unfinished murals, missing backdrops, undecorated trees, or were stuffed with unopened boxes of props, toys, and bags of false snow. Most troublesome, none of the animated figures were hooked up. Instead, they lay on the floor next to the nests of wire that brought them to life.

"What do we do?" Hector asked, running a hand through his hair again.

Stella slid out of Window #24 and dusted off her dress. "I have to finish, or I'll lose my job. My head too, Lord knows, if I disappoint the families in this city."

"*Your* head?" Hector pulled his glasses off and pocketed them. "Stells-Bells, you aren't alone in this." Hector's voice was the one un-Cary Grant-like thing about him. Grant spoke with a barky confidence. Hector's voice dropped soft and low when he was sincere, usually requiring Stella to lean in closer. "I had an entire press campaign built around Sal Sullivan," he whispered. "I'll have to completely reverse course—"

"Oh. Hi, Stella. Is Sal back there with you?" a shrill voice called.

Stella peeked around Hector to see Marjorie Hamm—a pale redhead with curls that reminded her of a twenty-something Shirley Temple—making her way down the corridor toward them.

Stella bristled. Out of all the store employees, Marjorie was the worst: a grade-A suck-up who possessed no talent, except her ability to kiss up to people. Stella saw through her like a Woolworth's tablecloth.

"Hi, Marjorie. Did you need something? You know we don't stock fur down here."

"Oh, no, I was looking for Sal, actually." Marjorie batted her eyes at Hector, as if he'd asked the question. "Have you seen him?"

"Dinner break," Hector coughed. He casually stepped in front of the window's open door, blocking Marjorie's view.

Stella raised her chin a little. She knew he felt the same way about Marjorie.

"Anything I can help you with?" Stella said.

"Oh, well, I was just hoping for a little peek at the windows. No need to get sore about it." Marjorie shrugged, batting her eyes at Hector. "As I was telling Ira in the elevator the other day, I'm swell at decorating. Of course, I'd already accepted the job in Furs when your position came up, Stella. But there's always next year, right?" Her lips twisted into a prissy smile.

"Really?" Stella felt the hot streak her dad swore she got from her Ukrainian mother's side of the family zip up her spine like a jolt of too-strong coffee. It would shock her into a grave if Ira could pick Marjorie out of a crowd.

"Well, the theme is still a secret." She crossed her arms. "The sidewalk outside Window Six would be an ideal place for you to wait on Saturday morning—"

Hector stepped in between them. "Marjorie, come to think of it, I passed a mink stole box just inside the door back there. Someone must've returned one last night. Won't you run it back upstairs? It would save me a trip."

Marjorie's smile drooped into a pout, getting the hint. "Sure, Hector." She gave Stella a once-over as she turned back and headed for the storeroom door. "Best of luck finishing, Stella. It's a huge responsibility. Huge."

Stella held perfectly still next to Hector, neither of them saying anything until they heard the door click.

"Ugh! She's such a tattle!" Stella bit her thumbnail. "Do you think she heard us?"

"No. But good ol' Hamm Hocks *would* interrupt Ira's Thanksgiving with that news. She'd swing in straight through the window like Tarzan just to tell on you. Glass shattering in his pumpkin pie and all!"

Stella pursed her lips, refusing to laugh. For a second, her eyes dropped to the cleft notched in Hector's chin.

Focus. Find help.

She turned and rushed back to Sal's desk.

"What do we do?" Hector said, trailing her.

"Find...someone." She sifted through Sal's mess, her mind whirling. She'd tell Ira about Sal the first chance she got, but he'd surely want to know what Stella was already doing to fix the problem.

"How's about Theodore Johns?" Hector suggested.

"He's doing Gimbel's floor display this year."

"Wilbur Sterling?"

"Horne's grabbed him."

"What about that costume designer? Ol' Dolores what's-her-name? The biddy with the glasses?"

"Filburn. And no, she's dressing The Nutcracker sets at Heinz Hall." Stella ran through other options in her head. "It's impossible to find a designer now. The reveal is just too close."

"Damn it." Hector slid out a second cigarette. "Sal was a big name for you. And a big story for me."

Stella dug through Sal's clutter until she found the folder she was looking for. Inside were the final *Home for the Holidays* sketches that Stella, Hector, and Sal (after Stella had dragged him out of the bar on Nine) had pitched to Ira months ago. It was a small relief, at least having the sketches that mapped out what props went where.

"What do we do?" Hector said.

She felt him take a step closer to her elbow, incredibly grateful for the "we." The situation felt like last year, when they worked in Customer Service together, and the occasional crisis would be on just the two of them to solve.

Stella and Hector had been hired at Hanover's on the same day, two holiday seasons ago, with Stella hoping to make enough to pay for college art classes without her dad's help. The first workday for all employees was spent down the street at McDuffy's School of Elocution & Etiquette where they learned proper manners and ways of greeting customers at the store. The instructor was Mrs. Alba McDuffy, a woman in her eighties who still wore high-necked dresses, carried an ancient parasol, and rolled her Rs when speaking. God love her, she was so stiff and proper. Without any drop of humor at all, she had no idea how hilariously stuffy she was.

It was McDuffy who'd paired Stella up with Hector to practice answering the telephone "with a proper smile" on their faces *and* in their voices.

"Hello, this is Hanover's Department Store. How may I be of assistance?" Stella had said through a plastered-on smile, blushing and feeling completely foolish as Hector, seated in the chair opposite her, took up a receiver and pretended to be the customer on the other end.

"Yes, this is Mr. J.P. Butterworth, millionaire," Hector had said in a faux-aristocratic accent. "I was wondering if you carried any caramels."

His fake accent was enough to make her laugh.

"I do r-r-r-require—" he kept on, starting to roll his Rs like McDuffy, "—at least one per night before bed."

"Just one caramel per night, Mr. Butterworth?" Stella struggled to keep her smile from turning into a laugh while McDuffy strolled behind Hector with one eyebrow raised.

"No, no, no. One whole *box* per night. You see I have a r-r-r-real sweet tooth that r-r-r-requires a good dose of sugar before bed."

"That's a lot of sugar."

"I do accompany it with a hearty glass of maple syrup. Do you sell that as well?"

He'd lifted his pinky finger on the hand holding the receiver, which was enough to send them both into a fit of laughter.

From then on, Hector could make Stella laugh with just a look. He'd been assigned to Men's Underwear but transferred two months later to work evenings with her in Customer Service. Shifts with Hector flew by, powered by giggles and coffee, and occasionally, caramels as a joke. If a customer had a problem—or *was* the problem—they'd solve it together. Six months later, Hector was promoted to press agent after a chance meeting with a newspaper editor who was desperate for help in choosing a birthday gift for his daughter. Their interaction landed the store an A-1 placement (which Stella learned was press talk for "front page"). Then when Ira began searching for a Head of Holidays, Hector had gotten some of Stella's sketch work in front him.

They were a great duo. The best. But Sal running out on them? This was their biggest crisis yet.

"What do we do?" Hector repeated.

Stella walked back toward the storeroom door, double-checking that Marjorie had really gone. As she did, her eyes caught on the *Buy War Bonds!* poster pinned to the back of the door.

"We rally the troops," Stella said, suddenly. "*Our* troops."

"What do you mean?"

She ran over it in her mind.

"Think about it. There are twelve floors of people out there who love this store just as much as we do. They spend every day helping people pick out the perfect gowns, the perfect jewels, the perfect gifts, right? So, we use the talent we have here."

"The sales staff?" Hector raised his eyebrows.

"Don't you dare, Mister Underwear," she warned. "Besides, you said yourself everyone else is taken. I need you to back me on this."

"Can we finish in time?"

Stella considered her alternatives. There were none.

"We'll grab some people—right now. If we start now, work all day tomorrow...even overnight if we have to... we can. We probably can. Yes. We will. Possibly?"

Hector's beautiful face looked horrified. "Well, that's a quote I will *not* be using in the press materials. We need muralists, Stel. Lighting designers. Machinists to get these gadgets working. Do you have a mechanic hiding out there in Sportswear, perhaps?"

"I may." She smirked, enjoying the look on Hector's face as she squinted at her wristwatch. "It's 7:40. Get out on that floor. Grab anyone who has a talent for, well, anything helpful. Meet me in the Bakery in fifteen minutes and bring them along—except Ol' Hamm Hocks. And Eleanor. We need people we can trust. At least until I can break the news to Ira."

"But Sal Sullivan was an award-winning designer. This is never going to work."

He slipped past her to hold the door for her. Always the gentleman.

"Hector, it has to."

Chapter 2

"Really, Stella, can you repeat that? My hearing's gone a bit silly!"

Luella from the Baby department blinked at Stella over her steaming cup of coffee at their table in Hanover's Bakery—a cozy place tucked in the back corner of the first floor. It, too, was closed for Thanksgiving, but the bakery staff was already banging around in the kitchen baking, from the smell of it, their city-famous pecan-raisin rolls for Friday morning.

"I'm serious. We need your help." She smiled at the group of six that she and Hector had managed to gather.

Stella's picks included John and Alfred, two bag-eyed carpenters dressed in dark blue overalls, who sat slumped in their chairs after finishing their final construction shifts in Santa's Village; middle-aged Joyce from Women's, who was a workhorse with a motherly demeanor, and steely-eyed Ruth, the store's long-time luxury stylist known for her great taste. Hector had naturally shown up flanked with two Santa Belles, high school-aged personal shoppers hired for the holidays. They sat, with flawless skin and hair styled into perfect victory curls (a style Stella could never seem to get her own wavy dark hair to agree to), giddy and giggling at the far end of the table.

"Here." Stella passed out the window sketches, distracted that the Belles kept shooting side glances toward Hector every few seconds. Hector didn't seem to notice. He only nodded at Stella to continue.

"We need— No..." Stella cleared her throat. "We *want* your help finishing this year's window displays."

Alfred twitched in his seat. "What do you mean our 'help'?"

"Well, we're in a bit of a bind," Stella began, sliding him the *Polar Christmas* sketch for Window #5.

"Where's Sal?" John asked, chewing on the end of what he'd been saving as his celebratory *Santa's Village is finished!* cigar. "Don't tell me that he left you holding the bag."

"Well. . ."

Alfred nodded his head in agreement. "Stella, I coulda told you he was rotten."

The brunette Santa Belle gasped. "*That* Sal? He was a chowderhead. He tried to pinch me in the elevator at least twice!"

Stella hurried to hand out more sketches. "Well, Sal is out, and I'm taking over. We've got to keep on and finish the job ourselves."

"But I've never done a window display before." Luella stared at Window #6's *Countryside Christmas* sketch. "Thousands of people walk by between now and Christmas. It's a big deal."

"But if you think about it, this group right here has all the skills that any good designer needs." Stella pointed to Ruth. "Excellent taste under pressure." She looked at Joyce. "A positive attitude." She waved at John and Alfred. "Experience building just about anything, right?"

"And willingness to learn," Hector gestured toward the Santa Belles, who shattered into giggles again.

Stella felt a wave of…what was it? Annoyance? Territorialism? pass through her. Clearly, they were clueless that Hector was going with Junie Clarke, a tall blonde that men referred to under their breaths as *a looker, a knockout, a doll*. Junie came from a well-off family who lived in one of the best neighborhoods in town, and was graceful enough to teach ballet to little girls on the weekends. The whole incident of how Stella had found out about Hector and Junie was an embarrassing nightmare that she'd hand over her life savings to forget.

Alfred leaned forward in his seat. "Just to be clear, *nothing's* been done yet?"

Stella winced and exchanged a look with Hector. He shrugged. She needed each one of them to help if this was going to work.

"*Almost* nothing."

John tossed his cigar on the table and rubbed his temples. "There are more than twenty windows, and what, less than three days? Santa's Village took two weeks to construct, two to decorate. You're asking us to do more than finish a job, Stella. You're asking us for a Christmas miracle!"

"'Tis the season," Hector quipped. The Belles giggled again.

"Well, you don't have to convince me." Joyce drummed her fingernails on the side of her coffee cup. "My husband proposed under the clock, right outside those windows at Christmastime. Besides, all five of my sons are overseas. I'd rather be where I'm needed."

Stella turned to Ruth. She stood five feet tall at most, with solid gray chin-length hair. She wore her clout like a cloak. Her reputation for having impeccable taste was legend in the city. No one would go up against Ruth. Definitely not Marjorie Hamm. Maybe not even Ira. If Stella could convince Ruth, she could get them all.

"What say you, Ruth?"

Ruth's ice blue eyes combed the sketches. Without looking up, she said, "Darling, I've dressed the Carnegies, the Fricks, and the Heinzes during my time here, times ten. Not to mention the pickiest brides in town. If I can dress them, I can dress anyone. Heaven knows a window will put up a lot less fuss."

"Wonderful!" Stella looked around the table. "Luella, you once mentioned you used to paint, right?"

"Well, yes. Paintings, not windows. But that was years ago."

"I'm just asking you to try." Stella pointed at the sketch in front of her. "*Countryside Christmas* needs a backdrop with a snowy meadow, a red barn, and evergreens."

"And that one's key. It will be photographed by all the papers during the big ribbon-cutting," Hector added, to which Stella shot him a look that said, *Don't you dare make her nervous.*

Luella clutched and re-clutched the handle of her beaded purse with her aged hands. "I brought my girls here for years to see the windows. The idea that my paintings would be in them, well, I suppose I could try."

"Great!" Stella pivoted toward the men, preparing herself to beg if need be. "John? Al? We can't do this without carpenters."

"I don't know, Stella." John ran a hand over his head, fluffing out his red hair that was fast fading to white. "We just finished the Village. Hazel's already sore at me for missing Thanksgiving dinner."

Hector butted in. "But if there are no windows to draw people into the store, no one will ever see your excellent village."

Stella held back a smile.

"Oh, don't be an old fuddy-duddy, John," Joyce said. "I'm in church choir with Hazel. She's crazy about Christmas. She'd love it!"

Stella glanced at the two Santa Belles. From the flirtatious smiles they aimed at Hector, she knew they'd need no convincing as long as he was around.

Hector grabbed her attention, tapping his watch as the others discussed it. He was right. If they were going to do this, they needed to start now. Enough haggling.

"Would overtime help?" Stella said. "For all of you?"

Alfred perked up. "How soon do we start?"

Stella braced herself. "Now."

Chapter 3

"And then instead of a ring coming with dessert, all she got was the orange sherbet she ordered, and she was *definitely* expecting a ring," the dark-haired Santa Belle hush-whispered to the other one with strawberry blonde hair. "She got heated and threw a fit, right there in the restaurant in front of everyone! They'd been going together almost a year. Can you imagine? She was sure they were gonna get hitched."

The friend wrinkled her nose. "She would act like that. She's so spoiled!"

Stella hung back, feeling awkward. She'd had Hector lead the group out of Hanover's Bakery and up toward the window access door at the front of the store while she gathered up the sketches and thanked the head baker for the coffee. She was just about to call ahead and ask the Santa Belles for their names when she'd realized they were gossiping just a few feet in front of her.

"Apparently that was the last straw for him," the dark-haired Santa Belle continued. "He broke things off with her that night."

"Jeez! When was this?"

"Last week. Now that he's single again, I betcha a malt I can get him to ask me out to a picture first," the brunette teased.

"Don't be dense," the strawberry blonde replied, tossing her hair. "If Junie's any example, Hector obviously likes blondes."

Junie? Hector?

"What?" Stella coughed, without meaning to.

The Belles turned, their faces going slack, then reddening as if they'd been caught doing something wrong.

They couldn't be talking about Hector and...Junie, could they?

The brunette Belle blushed, twisting her hands in front of her. "Oh, nothing. I was just saying that Hector...seems real swell. So do you, Miss West."

"Oh, yes. Real swell," the strawberry-blonde piped in, trying to save her friend. "Mina and I are happy to help with the windows, Miss West."

But Stella only nodded, ignoring her usual annoyance at being called "Miss." The Belles were only younger than she was by three or four years at most.

Had she heard them right? Hector is single? And he broke things off with Junie? Is he okay? Is he heartbroken? The thought made *her* feel heartbroken for a split second. What was wrong with her?

If truth be told, she couldn't say she was entirely sorry. Hector was one of her favorite people in the whole wide world, and well, Junie never really seemed to like her, which made for some very awkward run-ins. The few times Stella had been around the two of them, Junie seemed annoyed—even jealous—of the time she and Hector spent together at the store.

She trailed the group. Why wouldn't Hector tell her this? He told her everything else, didn't he? She knew his taste so well that she could order him lunch if he was running late. She knew he was embarrassed over his 4F status, because having polio when he was two years old had somehow disqualified him from enlisting in the war—especially since his older brother went and won a medal in only six months. She could tell by his face if he was in a good mood or bad, if he'd slept, if he'd drank too much or smoked too much, or if Ira had been giving him grief or praise (more often praise) over their latest newspaper coverage. She could tell exactly how funny he thought something was by the crookedness of his smile, and so many other things.

But all that was normal, right? When it came to a store this big, employees spent a lot of time together. They had to band together.

She felt guilt rush over her as she neared Fine Jewelry, wondering if Junie knew they often chose shifts so they could work together.

"Come on, Stells-Bells!" Hector called, holding the door for her as she was the last one in. He leaned down as she passed, close enough that Stella could smell his fresh pine aftershave.

"You know, I think this crazy plan of yours might work," he murmured.

"Mm-hmm," was all she could muster, her heart suddenly fluttering.

The sight of so many unpacked boxes sent Stella's mind plummeting back to the dilemma at hand. She jumped into divvying out responsibilities: Windows #1 and #2 were done. John and Alfred would unpack the props for Windows #3 and #4, and then pass them to Mina and Shirley—the strawberry blonde Belle—to set up inside. Stella would take Window #5, *Polar Christmas*.

Luella would start on the mural in Window #6, *Country-side Christmas*. Joyce would go window-by-window and take an inventory of what was there (or missing) based on the sketches.

Ruth took one glance at the plans for Window #12, *Heavenly Christmas*—a window strung with angel dolls with jeweled wings—and declared it the most beautiful. She announced that she'd take care of it.

Once everyone else was in place, Stella hurried to Window #5. Hector followed her inside the window display.

"So, where does this little guy go?" He tipped his chin toward one of the unwrapped penguins that lay like mummies at his feet.

Stella studied the sketch. *Polar Christmas* was to feature an igloo backdrop and a frosty pond where penguins slid over the ice.

"First, we need to lay the pond and hang the backdrop. Then we can set the figures up."

The round mirror that was to serve as the frozen pond was pinned against the wall behind Hector by stacked boxes. He maneuvered it to the center of the window display, rolling it on its side like a wheel.

"Whatever you do, don't drop it," Stella said, grabbing the other end.

"Oh, you don't have to tell me. We can't afford more bad luck!"

They slowly flipped it horizontally and lowered it to the ground. Grooves had been carved in the middle of it for the figures to move.

"Perfect. Now, I think the backdrop is...there." Stella pointed to a scrim rolled up like a giant tube of wrapping paper propped in one corner. "But we need to glue it to the back wall somehow."

She unrolled it as Hector loosened his tie. He shrugged off his suit jacket, then folded up his sleeves. She felt her cheeks flush. She glanced around the crowded window, suddenly aware that this was the tightest space she and Hector had been in in months. It felt oddly intimate with everyone else locked away in their windows.

What was going on with her? They'd been alone plenty of times before.

Suddenly, the news of Hector and Junie was gnawing her.

"Can we nail it?" he asked, staring down at the backdrop.

"No, it's a bit heavy. Nails would tear through it. We need some kind of glue."

She leaned down toward the window door. "Hey, Alfred? John? Got any heavy-duty paste out there?"

"For what?" Alfred yelled as the tune of "White Christmas" started up. Alfred must've brought down his portable victrola. He'd played music constantly during the installation of Santa's Village to pass the time.

"We have to secure an igloo backdrop to the wall." Stella picked up one corner. It felt like wallpaper but thicker.

Alfred stuck his head in the window's tiny door, peering at it. "Wallpaper paste would do it."

"Got any in Hardware?"

"I can check." He disappeared back into the hall, and she and Hector were alone again.

"Here." Stella picked up a box of glass icicle ornaments that were to frame the whole scene around the window. "We can at least hang these while we wait." She unfolded a stepladder propped against one wall. "I'll climb. You hand them to me."

He crinkled his brow, eyeing the rungs on the ladder. "You sure? I'm taller, and besides, you have a penchant for...incidents."

She kicked off her pumps and climbed up. "Is that a nice way to call me clumsy?"

Hector gave her a half-smile. "*Is* there a nice way to call you clumsy?" He strung clear fishing line through the hooks on the icicles and passed them up to her.

She climbed another two steps, stretched up, and hooked them onto a rack that framed the inside of the window for just this purpose.

"Say, I feel like I haven't seen you in weeks," Hector said, tearing open another box of icicles.

"You haven't. My new address is 'Santa's Village, Hanover's, Fifth Floor'."

"Sounds enchanting. How's it look?"

"Perfect. That's one thing done." She sighed. "I just wish I would've paid more attention here, too."

"You can't blame yourself. Sal was supposed to be a pro." His fingertips brushed hers as he passed her another handful of icicles.

Stella's mind turned back to Hector and Junie.

Don't fish. Don't do it. Don't.

She bit her bottom lip, stringing up the next icicles. "How 'bout you? Anything new?"

Damn it. She felt a butterfly-like flutter rush through her chest. She wanted to know if the news of their breakup was true. But if it wasn't true, she *really* didn't want to know.

"Busy, like you," he said, passing her more icicles. "This press plan has been killing me, but, boy, will it be worth it if we...you know...have windows to unveil on Saturday."

"We'll finish. It may not be perfect, but we'll do it."

He handed her another. "Say, is your dad going to make it to the reveal? I can save a seat for him in the VIP section."

She smiled, knowing Hector was going to love her answer. "Not on Saturday. He's driving Ol' Tillie in the parade, so. . ."

His entire face lit up. "Ah, Ol' Tillie? He'll have the best seat yet, then."

Hector was obsessed with fact that Stella's dad was a fireman, and his fascination only grew after meeting him back in July when his birthday gift caused a debacle outside the store.

Stella had brought her dad to the store to pick out a new armchair for his present. He'd dressed up in his Sunday suit with his green vest underneath for the occasion. He was the vision of a perfect Irishman and had run around introducing himself to everyone as Stella's "da." For his gift, he'd chosen a smart brown leather chair with a button-tufted back—but after twenty sweltering minutes trying to fit it into the backseat of their car under the blazing sun, Stella, dad, (and Hector, who'd offered to help) stood on the sidewalk, resigned to the fact that it was indeed too big.

"I really don't mind paying for delivery, Dad," Stella had said, casually trying to wipe sweat off her upper lip without Hector noticing. "It's only ten dollars more."

"Bah! That's a whole day's pay!" He'd waved the suggestion away.

"I still say we could tie it to the roof." Hector dabbed his brow with a handkerchief. Why was it that the sweat on his brow added a dreamy sheen to his face, while Stella felt like a sweaty mess?

Dad ran his hand over the chair's leather, looking pained. "She's a beaut. We can't risk this dirty city air mucking her up."

"Could you borrow a truck? Maybe a neighbor has one?" Hector suggested.

Stella squinted, thinking. "Everyone I know takes the trolley. . ."

"Ha, I've got it!" Her dad clapped his hands. "Stella, wait here with the chair, will ya? Hector, you come along."

"Wait, where are you going?" Stella said, standing on the sidewalk, feeling a little jilted.

But he didn't say a word, only smiled wide enough for the gap in his two front teeth to show. Dad hopped in the car and waved at Hector to join him. Hector looked at Stella, surprised, as he climbed into the passenger seat before the two drove off.

Stella had waited on the sidewalk with the chair for fifteen minutes, wondering what the brilliant idea was, until Ol' Tillie—the fire company's hook and ladder—appeared at the top of the hill and sped down toward her. Her dad was in the driver's seat with Hector next to him, grinning like a wicked little boy. Stella froze, equal parts shocked and embarrassed, trying not to laugh at the same time.

Cars swerved around the fire truck as they pulled over to park by the sidewalk.

"Christ on a bike, Dad!" she'd said as soon as he'd cracked his door.

"Ah, we're only a bit on the fiddle. Ol' Tillie's hungry for a proper fill-up." He'd patted her hood. "We'll be sure to get her a full tank on the way back. Right, Hector?"

Hector had marched past Stella, carrying a tarp and shaking his head in disbelief. "Don't look at me, I'm just the helper here." He unrolled the tarp over the chair.

"More like co-conspirator," Stella said. "What if there's a fire?!"

"All the more reason to help us get this loaded up and on our way," Dad said.

She'd rushed to help them wrap the chair in the tarp and tie it up top, then had sat squashed in between her dad and Hector in Ol' Tillie's front seat—her thigh against Hector's the whole way home.

In the end, Ol' Tillie never did get a fill-up, but the chair made it safely to their living room. Hector had recounted the incident, excitedly, for weeks.

Stella strung up the last icicle. "Last one here. I think I'm done."

"Stella!" Alfred yelled from the hall, following up with a rap on their window door. "Wallpaper paste! Come on out!"

They retreated into the corridor, where the Belles had also gathered to get paste for their backdrops.

"Now that's a lovely color," Hector grimaced at the two buckets of what looked like thick booger-colored goo that John was stirring with a paintbrush.

"Does it have to smell so bad?" Mina said, pinching her nose.

"You don't have to love it. Just slap some on, wait five full minutes, then stick it on the wall and hold it there for about five more minutes," Alfred instructed, passing Mina a bucket and brush. He handed the other to Hector, who turned his face away.

Stella climbed back inside, and the two moved two penguin figures aside to make enough room to flip the igloo on its back.

"Wow, this really stinks." Hector wiped on the paste.

"As long as it does its job, I don't care." Stella moved the ladder to the back of the window.

"That should do it." Hector sat back. "Five minutes?"

The upturned igloo had taken almost all their floor space, and Stella wasn't going to chance opening anything and getting stinky glue on any of their mostly white polar decorations. She sat down on a ladder rung.

"Got plans for the holidays yet?"

Hector jammed his hands in his pockets and looked around. "Other than spending Thanksgiving in here?"

"I meant Christmas." And there she was, fishing for information on Junie again.

"No plans yet. I'll visit my mom at some point, but she's still a bit down with my brother away."

"How is he?"

"The war hero?" He scratched behind his ear. "Wonderful. We get a letter from him every few weeks, but that's it."

Stella stooped down to gather up the empty icicle boxes, knowing not to push him on his brother. Any mention of servicemen rattled Hector's attitude toward his disqualification.

Don't do it. Don't.

"No other plans? No dinner or drinks?"

He shrugged. "I'm kind of terrible at planning ahead when it comes to those things."

"Mm." She took a breath.

No.

"Junie isn't planning anything for you two?" she blurted, at the same time Hector asked, "Say, what's that sound?"

"Huh?" Stella froze from gathering the boxes, not knowing who spoke first. Hector looked at her with raised eyebrows, as if waiting for her to respond. Had he not heard her, or was he trying to change the subject?

A second passed. He still looked like he was waiting on her.

"Do you hear it? There's a scratching sound."

"No. What sound?"

He raised a finger, beckoning her over to where he stood, then put his finger to his lips in a silent *shh!* motion.

She stepped over and held perfectly still, listening.

"Hear that? I've heard it a few times now."

She shook her head. *Nothing. Wait, no, maybe a tiny scratch?* She locked eyes with Hector as they both listened.

Standing this close, she could see he was getting a five o'clock shadow. He was handsome. More handsome than Cary Grant, she decided. Grant wasn't funny. Hector was very funny.

She jumped a little as he reached up and pulled a strand of icicle packing material from her hair.

Suddenly, it felt like the space was closing in on them. Why? They'd been alone plenty. Lots of shifts.

Lots of shifts. When he was going with Junie. And unavailable.

"Probably just someone passing outside," she mumbled. It felt like it was a hundred degrees in there. She took a step back, stooped down, and tested the tackiness of the glue with her fingers. "Hey, I think this is ready to stick."

She hurried for the ladder and set it up in place.

Maybe she should just admit what she'd overheard from the Santa Belles and ask if it was true.

Hector paused. "Are you sure you should—"

"I'll be fine. Just pass the top up to me."

Hector lifted up the edge and carefully passed it to Stella so that the sticky side was facing her. All she had to do was stick it to the top of the wall, then press it down.

"So, like I was saying," she continued, "has Junie planned anything for—"

"Wait, wait! Freeze!" Hector said, looking at the backdrop from the other side. "We've got it backwards. Look. The igloo is upside down."

"It can't be up—" Stella had leaned forward to peek over the top of it, but she'd leaned too far.

Her heel slipped straight off the ladder rung. She crashed down, falling forward, landing chest-first into the sticky side of the igloo, and barreling into Hector. He caught himself on the clean side of the backdrop, while Stella slipped down onto her hands and knees on the gooey side.

She landed on the ground on all fours.

Neither of them moved for a second.

"Ugh! Oh, yuck!" Stella peeled herself back covered with glue.

"Stella? What—" Hector got to his feet, his mouth covered with one hand. His eyes widened and his shoulders shook like he was desperate to hold a laugh in. "What did you do? Are you okay? Is your foot okay?"

She felt her face flush beet red as she kicked off her remaining shoe and stood up. The entire front of her dress was covered with glue that stunk like rubber and chemicals.

She would've covered her face with her hands, if they weren't saturated with glue, too. She was so embarrassed.

"I'm fine, I'm just...covered with...gosh this stuff stinks!"

Hector erupted.

"Laugh it up. Laugh it up." She stood, pinching the sides of her ruined dress. "Are you okay at least?"

"Well, you did drop an igloo on me." Hector stepped back and laid the backdrop out, glue side up, over the pond. "Why don't I...get one of the girls to help you? You're going to have to change, or everything's going to stick to you. I'll have Joyce or Mina come help."

Hector snuck past her and slipped out into the hall. Stella stood there, sticky and dripping and praying none of it was in her hair.

She wanted to die. And worse, she'd completely botched her chance to find out about Hector and Junie.

Seconds later, the window's door cracked open. Joyce peered in sideways. Thank goodness he'd grabbed her and not one of the perfect Santa Belles.

"Oh, Stella." Joyce covered her mouth. "You've gotten yourself into a real pickle, haven't you? I'm sorry, but I can't help but laugh."

"I'm fine. I just want this stuff off of me. Did I get any in my hair?"

Joyce squinted. "No, not that I see. Take off your dress. I'll run and get a new one for you to change into."

"Right here?"

Joyce glanced back in the corridor behind her. "You want to chance trailing that goop everywhere?"

"Good point."

Joyce snapped the window door shut. Stella undid her belt.

"Mina? Come guard this door," Joyce hollered. "No one gets in but me."

"Why? What's happened?" Mina called from down the corridor.

"Stella's spilled glue all over herself. She needs a change of clothes."

"She did *what*?"

Good lord, stop talking about it.

"If I could just get that new dress—" Stella interrupted.

"How's about I stand down here and make sure no one accidentally bumps the curtain switch?" Hector called from a few windows down, referring to the master switch across from Window #1 that opened all the curtains on each window in the series.

Stella groaned, unzipping. "Careful, Hector Donovan. I dropped an igloo on you once. I'll do it again!"

His laughter disappeared down the hallway.

Stella let her dress fall to the ground. She stepped out of it, standing there in only her slip. Then she balled the dress up, the goo-side gathered in the center, she wiped her hands on it and placed it by the window door.

She nudged the igloo back off the edge of the mirrored pond and checked her reflection to confirm no glue had made it into her hair. Stella had her mother's Ukrainian features: dark hair, the same dark eyes, and heavy brows. Her fair skin and freckles came from her dad's Irish side.

She wished she'd inherited her mother's figure.

Stella crossed her arms over her chest, feeling ridiculous. This Hector thing was too distracting. How was it possible that "the store's first-ever Head of Holidays" was so wrapped up in a rumor that she was now standing in a shop window in just her slip? Of course, it wasn't even her good slip. It was her comfy slip with the missing bit of lace at the knee. And she still had that bruised thigh from before.

She'd just started shivering when Hector called over the wall again.

"You surviving in there?" he asked. Mina must've abandoned her post.

The sound of his voice suddenly made Stella very aware that she was nearly naked, or at least as close to naked as she'd ever been standing just feet away from a man before.

"Yes." She walked toward the wall, her bare feet sneaking through the spill. "Trying not to freeze to death, no pun intended."

"That would make an interesting headline."

She smiled. It was Hector's favorite game, one they used to play on slow nights, making up newspaper pitches on how they'd saved the store from difficult customers.

"How's about, 'Woman Freezes to Death After Igloo Accident in Downtown Pittsburgh'? I could sell that," he said.

"Ha ha." Stella glimpsed at the mirror again, feeling Hector's presence on the other side of the wall. She studied herself, wondering if he'd ever go for a girl like her, or if he had a type like the Belles said he did. If Junie had set any standard, he liked tall blonde ballerinas. Not short Ukrainian brunettes who could no longer argue they weren't the biggest klutz in town.

"Shoo, Hector! Help is here, dear!" Joyce knocked on the door. "I grabbed a dress. Your waist is what, twenty-eight inches, I'm guessing? Twenty-nine?"

Ugh. Of course she'd yelled that right in front of Hector. Junie was probably a twenty-four-inch waist at most.

"I'll make it work." Stella flattened her back against the wall and grabbed the bundle Joyce's arm snaked in through the door, trying to be discrete. She shook it out. It was a hideous brown dress the color of a paper bag with charcoal lace detailing across the chest.

Fantastic. She made a face, thinking staying covered in glue might be more attractive.

Not wanting to waste any more time, she hurried it up over her waist and slipped her arms through. Then she sucked in her belly and hopped around, trying to zip herself.

New mission: quit fooling around. Find out the truth about Hector and Junie so you can stop obsessing over it and move on. No matter if the rumor is true or not.

She could move on no matter what, right?

Chapter 4

For the next few hours, Stella and Hector barely had a moment to speak to each other. Stella repeatedly got pulled away to answer questions and help track down rogue props. Her calves ached from running up and down that damn escalator to grab Luella more paint, or John and Alfred more supplies from Hardware.

When there wasn't something to do, she helped the Santa Belles finish up Windows #3 and #4, secretly hoping they'd spill more about Hector. Instead, they treated her like an old schoolmarm, not that she could blame them. She looked like one in that hideous brown dress.

Hector, on the other hand, had been snapped up by John and Alfred on the mere fact that he was a man. The three of them were lifting the heaviest boxes, while Joyce directed which props belonged in which window.

The group called it quits at 11:00 p.m., just in time to get their coats and run for the last trolleys out of downtown. Hector and a few of the others promised to meet Stella at 6:00 a.m. the next morning. Hanover's didn't open until nine, so they would be able to get a lot of work done before anyone's shift started. The others promised to stop in during their breaks or join after their work. Alfred, who technically had Friday off, promised

Stella (with overtime written all over his face) to stay for the long haul.

Stella boarded the Number Four trolley carrying her ruined dress in a bag and slumped into a seat in the empty third row. She leaned her head against the dark window, exhausted by everything. The group had finished four more of the twenty-six windows tonight, which left them twenty to complete in a little more than twenty-four hours—a number that made her shudder. Plus, there were the electronic figures. They hadn't even begun looking at how to wire them.

And the whole Hector and Junie thing still bothered her—but it bothered her more why it mattered so much to her. Sure, there was a time right after she started working with Hector that she thought maybe they might be sort of perfect for each other *outside* of the store. She'd even dropped hints (actually, hint after hint) that she really wanted to see the new Alfred Hitchcock movie that was coming out, weeks before opening night. But then a blonde swanned through the door of Customer Service late one night, ignoring Stella's greeting and immediately reaching for Hector's hand. He'd introduced Junie to Stella as his girl and that was that. Stella had felt so foolish at the time, she could still feel how it burned to see Junie grab his hand, all smiles.

But she'd put those feelings aside months ago, hadn't she?

Stella picked at a stray thread on her glove. Maybe her feelings for Hector weren't gone entirely.

Perhaps she could ask Mina for the full story tomorrow? No, that would be silly. And unprofessional. And giggly girls like the Santa Belles could always tell what a girl was really asking. Giggly girls know more than anyone.

Of course, Stella didn't have many girlfriends her own age to ask their opinion either. Most of her high school friends were married with at least one baby by now. Some were already having their second. The ones who were once giggly, weren't anymore. Most of them just looked exhausted. Even the book Stuffy McDuffy had given her and all the other women in her Elocution & Etiquette training class, *Courtesy in Courting: Guidelines for Men and Women*, had been printed fifteen years ago. None of the rules applied today.

War also seemed to have changed everything, too. Mina had dropped her bet with Shirley about getting Hector to ask her out. She'd reviewed for a good hour the number of boys she had abroad writing to her—which only made it clear to Stella exactly how hard it was to meet a good, single man now. For girls as young as Mina and Shirley, flirtation, commitment, and promises were all made via letter to boys they went to high school with or knew from the neighborhood or church. Forget meeting anyone new. And who really knew how many boys the girls were writing to at one time—and vice versa? Stella felt bad for the Belles really, never having had the chance to get asked by a boy to go to a picnic or to see a picture show in person, or to kiss a boy and not worry that they wouldn't see him again for months.

Not that Stella had a deep romantic history of her own. Her last relationship had cooled the week after high school ended, with little heartbreak on either part. (He'd been a decent high school baseball player, but after baseball season ended, he was all too excited to share his other passion with Stella: bird watching. She'd ended things after listening to a less-than-riveting hour-long explanation of the color patterns of blue jays).

Stella sighed as the trolley rumbled past her dad's fire station, suddenly feeling like the igloo was a metaphor for her own love life. Cold. Lonely. Immobile.

Chapter 5

Just before midnight, Stella made her way inside the snug two-bedroom apartment she still shared with her dad and tossed her coat over the kitchen chair. He had left the lamp on in the next room and the radio hummed low. Stella quietly placed her keys on the kitchen table, doing her best to not make noise.

Her stomach rumbled. When was the last time she'd eaten? She backtracked to the icebox and popped it open to see her dad had left her a plate of two turkey legs, peas, and biscuits. She swore up and down that peas tasted like wet cardboard, but right now she was too hungry to care. She pulled out the plate, then poured herself a glass of water, just as dad limped into the kitchen, squinting as he flipped on the light.

"Happy Thanksgiving, Stella. Sorry. I tried to stay up." He squeezed her shoulder. "Jesus, Mary, and Joseph, it's nearly midnight. You must be knackered. There's really that much to do at the store, yeah?"

"Ugh. Yes." She plunked down into the kitchen chair and bit into one of the turkey legs, too hungry to tell the tale.

He poured himself a glass of milk, then sat down across from her.

"Why do you smell like smoke?" she asked, swallowing faster than she could chew.

"Thanksgiving's a banner day for fires, I'll tell ya." He took a sip. "Plenty of bleedin' ejits settin' their houses on fire."

Stella stopped. "You didn't go out on any calls, did you? You were supposed to have dinner with Ms. Maureen. Your knee—"

"Oh, I showed for dinner." He nodded to her plate. "Then I stopped into the station for a bit. Just to field the telephones." He ran a hand over his knee. "Besides, my leg's nearly healed. I'll be fine any day now."

"You know what the doctor said."

"Ejit! Too young a fella. What does he know? He probably hasn't seen a day of hard work in his life. It's a gammy knee is all." He drained his glass. "If this was Dublin, I'd still be on the job."

"Dad, he took an x-ray. And besides, you don't need to worry about working right now. Not with my new job. I can pay the bills for as long as you need."

Her dad stared at his empty glass as he slid it back and forth on the tabletop. "That's not how things should be though, Stella. I'm your *da*. Providing for you is my job. I'll work the phones until this is better. Silly fool I am. More than forty fires over the years, and in the end, I make a holy show out of tripping over a hose!" He ran his hand over his knee again.

"You want to hear about a silly fool, I can beat that." Stella hurried through the story of Sal running off, the igloo incident, and the immense job that lay in front of her.

"By Jesus, that takes the biscuit." He folded his arms across his chest and leaned back in his chair. "Your mother loved those windows. Damn near every year she'd sew you a new outfit, a fancy red or green for the holidays. We'd take the trolley, stand in that crowd no matter the rain or the snow."

"I'm worried we won't finish in time," Stella admitted, shoveling her spoon into the peas.

Her dad pushed himself to his feet with a groan. "You'll finish. You got too much of your mother's fight in you to not."

Stella swallowed, hoping he was right.

FRIDAY

Chapter 6

Stella stared at the words on the front page of the day's paper as her trolley shimmied back toward downtown. Hector, the publicity wizard he was, had nailed his job of nabbing front-page coverage. This year's addition of having Santa disembark his float at the end of the parade and unveil Hanover's windows himself was genius. A true win for Hector's reputation. But that made Stella feel even more uneasy that so much work lay ahead of them.

She smoothed down her black coat. This morning, she'd chosen her favorite dress—a long-sleeved forest green one, tight at the waist, that flared out below the knee. She hoped it would give her a kick of confidence after winding up in that hideous brown dress the night before. She'd pulled her wavy hair half-back with bobby pins, added a touch of red lipstick, and a tiny dab of

Rose Bulgare perfume to her wrists (Stella had splurged on a bottle before it was printed in all the Hollywood magazines that Ava Gardener wore it and Hanover's was sold out for months).

After a night of mediocre sleep, she'd woken up steeped in the realization that she was still attracted to Hector. Maybe very attracted to Hector. But she had to guard her heart. She refused to hold these feelings in her mind too long just in case the rumor wasn't true.

Still, she wondered if Hector would notice her touched-up look.

Stella folded up the newspaper and watched the dark accordion of row houses that lined the streets in their part of town stretch into churches, then into storefronts. She tried to remember the last Christmas they'd come to see the windows as a family of three, when her mother was still alive. She had visions of them standing outside Hanover's windows, exhaling steamy breaths, and squeezing one another's hands with excitement until it was their turn at the front of the line.

"I hope Daddy and I can buy you a beautiful dress just like that one someday," her mother had said, lifting her up. She'd pointed to a white dress with gold trim on a mannequin on the other side of the glass. "Maybe I'll make you one like that for Christmas."

Stella couldn't remember how old she was, just that she was old enough to still be carried and that the dress was white.

"It looks like a dress an angel would wear," she remembered her mother saying.

One week later, her mother had gotten sick enough to stay in bed. She'd stayed there through Christmas. Then through New Year's.

And then, after a few more weeks, on a cold snowy morning, Stella's mother became an angel herself.

Some kind of cancer. Her dad didn't like talking about it.

Stella stared out the window and debated what to do about Ira as the trolley rounded into the financial section of downtown. She certainly couldn't keep this a secret from him. With it being the day after Thanksgiving, he'd most certainly be back at the store today. She decided to go to him first thing, tell him about Sal leaving them in a lurch, then share what she'd been doing to solve the problem—and pray to Jesus, Mary, *and* Joseph that he didn't fire her.

She rested back in her seat and let the decision settle over her. Yes. Talking to Ira would make her feel better. She had done the best she could in a bad situation, hadn't she? He couldn't fault her for that. And he couldn't fire her either, right? Like Stella, Ira literally didn't have time to find a replacement.

So, goals for the day: finish windows, talk to Ira, and don't get fired. And find a definitive answer on the status of Hector and Junie.

She was still picking out exactly what to say to Ira when the trolley stopped at the corner of Penn Avenue and Smithfield Street. Outside, Stella spotted a small, excited crowd gathering in the dark, pointing up at something.

What would cause a crowd at this hour?

Her heart jumped. She shot to her feet.

"Wait!" Stella called to the driver before he could close the door.

She hurried off and stared straight up at the building on the corner. Shining right there, in its fifty-foot-tall glory, was the Joseph Horne's Co. department store Christmas tree—lit up a full day earlier than advertised.

Stella jumped up onto the curb as the trolley clanged behind her and sped away.

The fake evergreen was cleverly wrapped around the corner of the Horne's building, drawing attention of shoppers walking down two of the busiest streets in the city's retail district. This year, the tree sported strands of gold garland and red-and-white ornaments shaped like diamonds.

Christ on a bike. Ira's going to combust.

A man in an expensive coat paused beside her and regarded it as well.

"Old Horne's really did it again, eh? Looks bigger than last year's, too!"

He was right, Stella realized, by at least a yard or so, and it had more ornaments than she could count.

She glanced at her watch. 6:04 a.m. Stella needed to catch Ira before anyone else, certainly before he heard about their biggest competitor's tree debuting early.

She turned down the block and sped on foot toward Hanover's.

Hector was waiting for her under the clock outside the store, cigarette in hand. The massive century-old Victorian timepiece was already dressed up for the season with fresh evergreens and holly around its face. The "Clock on the Corner" was a city landmark in itself: Shoppers would often enter Hanover's and divide up, promising to meet under the clock when they were done. It was also where guys and gals met up for dates downtown and kissed goodnight when the day was over.

Hector appeared to be deep in conversation with the corner's shoe shiner, who was setting up for the day.

He winked at her as she crossed the street toward him. Then his eyes ticked down to Stella's red lipstick for a split second.

Her heart fluttered. Hector had winked at her before, hadn't he?

He excused himself and stepped away, leading Stella toward the front door.

"Did Cece catch you?" he asked before she could get a word out.

"Cece?" The fact that Ira's secretary was looking for her couldn't be good. "No. Why?"

"She telephoned me when she couldn't get you. Ira wants a preview of the windows this morning. For him and the governor."

They were standing so close that Stella could tell he'd just shaved. And he smelled like toothpaste and fresh aftershave. It felt strange having just seen him so late at night and then again so early in the morning. Private. Intimate even.

Focus. Stella blinked, repeating, "The governor?"

"A late addition to the plan. He's supposed to help Santa Claus with the ribbon-cutting tomorrow. Apparently, he came in early to avoid weather in Philadelphia," Hector said, stamping out his cigarette. "Ira's having breakfast with him over at his hotel at seven-thirty. Cece asked what time would be good for them to drop by."

"Oh my god!" Stella rifled in her handbag for her key. "Well, that's it. I'm going to get fired. We're not even half-way done. I haven't had a chance to talk to him about Sal. And now Horne's—"

Hector straightened. "What's about Horne's?"

"You didn't take the trolley in?"

"I sprang for a taxi as soon as Cece called. Why?"

She grimaced. "The tree is up a day early."

"Holy mackerel!" Hector ran one hand through his hair. "Is it—"

"Fabulous? There's already a small crowd. What are we going to do?"

Just then, a *pop!* like a tiny gunshot, echoed from up the street, jolting them both. Stella looked past Hector to see one of the store's Delivery Fleet trucks parked in the alley around the far corner of the store. A blue-uniformed delivery boy was staring underneath its smoking hood while another shouted instructions from the driver's seat.

"Wait! I have an idea," Stella said, squeezing Hector's shoulder and rushing to the truck.

The Delivery Fleet was another new addition for the holidays. Dozens of local boys, old enough to drive but too young to enlist, had been hired as a part of the store's "free delivery anytime, anywhere" sales gimmick Ira had come up with. Of course, the first day the ad ran, some fathead in Toledo, Ohio had telephoned in an order for a gallon jug of Heinz ketchup. It took the sixteen-year-old driver two days and four maps to get there and back.

Hector, naturally, had turned it into a winner of a story for the papers.

"That should do it. Try the ol' clunker again."

Stella walked up to a lanky boy with fair hair and a slightly too-big uniform waving to the driver. She watched as the boy peered into the engine. It revved again, then squealed before sputtering out.

"Excuse me—"

The boy straightened himself and adjusted his jacket. "Oh, sorry about the racket, ma'am. We've almost got her going. She can take a while to start when it's this cold out."

"Oh, quite all right! See, I work for the store. We're looking for a few mechanically minded individuals to help with...a special project."

"What kind of project?" asked the boy behind the wheel, leaning out the window.

She exchanged a look with Hector, then looked back at the two of them. "Mind following me?"

"It's no wonder nothin's workin', ma'am. Your master switch and circuit board are as black as burnt toast," Billy said. That was the name of the fair-haired Delivery Fleet boy who was now lying on his belly, peering into a crawl space beneath Window #1. His friend crouched next to him, holding a flashlight.

"What's a circuit board?" Stella whispered to Hector, who shrugged.

"It's the power center that holds all the wires together. It helps everything turn on or off," the friend answered as Billy shimmied out.

"That explains why nothing's working," Hector said.

"Can you fix it?" Stella asked.

"Maybe?" Billy's eyes flitted to his friend. "We'd pretty much need to replace the whole thing. I haven't done it before, but I've read about it lots."

Stella put her hands on her hips. "Say, do you think you two, maybe even some of the other Delivery Fleet boys, could help out in here in between your deliveries? Not just with the wires, but with the windows in general? We need a lot of props put together and set up."

"Well," Billy glanced at his friend. "We haven't had any orders come in yet today. I wouldn't mind staying in here. It's freezing out!"

"We could take turns," the friend suggested. "I'll go back to the truck. Come get me if an order comes in, and we'll swap."

"Bless you!" Stella said. The storeroom door cracked open behind them.

"Good morning!" It was Joyce, followed by Mina and Shirley, early just like they'd promised.

The delivery boys' jaws nearly dropped at the sight of the girls, who were dressed in their Santa Belle getups: form-fitting green dresses and red sequined caps.

Stella gestured at the Delivery Fleet boys. "We have new helpers today."

"Ah, more help is always welcome!" Joyce said as she unwound her scarf.

Mina smiled at Billy, whose ears turned beet red.

"Well, let's get to it," Stella said. Hector handed her the sketches from Sal's desk.

She continued. "Windows Three and Four are as done as they can be until we figure out the animated figures. Mina and Shirley, can you finish up *A Kitchen Christmas* in Window Seven? That one has a mechanical mouse celebrating Christmas by eating gingerbread men and candy canes. And Joyce, can you start unpacking Window Eight? It's a *Gnome Glen* full of gnomes and little furry creatures. Anything electronic, just unwrap and set aside for the moment. Hector and I will take Window Nine, *Santa's Toyshop*. It's mostly toys. We should get that one done pretty quick."

They all nodded and hurried to their windows. Mina threw another smile to Billy, then bounced down the corridor behind Joyce.

Luella arrived just then—Alfred and John holding the door for her.

Stella hurried a greeting, then explained Billy's finding of the ruined circuit board to the men. They did an about-face and headed up to Hardware to look for replacement parts.

"Think you'll be able to finish this morning, Luella?" Stella asked, walking with her to Window #6.

"Oh, yes. You know, I think it will be lovely." The corner of her eyes crinkled as she smiled. "If I could just get the snow to frost my evergreens just so...I brought my old brushes today." She patted her pocketbook.

Stella nodded, stepping back as Hector helped Luella step up.

"It will be lovely, if she's able to finish the darn thing," Hector whispered after she was safely inside.

Stella elbowed him in the ribs as they continued to Window #9. "She's doing her best."

"You should've assigned her a glacier at the rate she paints," he grinned. "A glacier would go well with, what... an igloo? Wait, no. Igloos are rather risky business."

"Stop teasing." Stella pushed past him and reached for the telephone. She dialed as Hector leaned on Sal's desk next to her. "I need Cece to stop Ira from coming by. I don't want to tell him his window designer ran off in front of the governor."

But there was no pickup at Cece's extension.

"Damn it." She put the phone down.

"Well, I can help until the run-through with Martin this afternoon," Hector said.

Stella slid a hand up to her forehead. "I totally forgot about that. That is today, isn't it?"

Martin Clark had played Santa Claus at the store for at least ten years. He was a former stage actor and was fantastic at playing Santa but was also very particular about rehearsing his part and knowing exactly how to maximize the crowd's reaction.

Hector tapped his watch. "He'll be here at four, so we better get started."

Stella turned the sketch of Window #9 toward Hector. "This one shouldn't take too long, see—"

Just then the door cracked.

"Is *Signorina* Stella in here?" a man's voice said.

Stella's heart jumped thinking it was Ira, then steadied when she realized *signorina* could only come from one person: Gio, the young assistant baker at Hanover's Bakery.

Straight from Naples, Gio.

Gio had always openly drooled over Stella and wouldn't stop asking her on dates...in the most uncomfortable ways. The worst part was that he was so nice. Overtly nice. *Awkwardly* nice. She was happy to be kind in return, but he never seemed to get the hint when a conversation was over. Or that she wasn't interested in going to see a picture show or walk through a park with him, which made every interaction with him more than a bit awkward.

Gio shuffled in through the doorway backwards with a tray of breakfast rolls and a pitcher of coffee and mugs balanced against his chest. His thick glasses slipped down the bridge of his beak-like nose.

"Buongiorno, buongiorno to everybody!" Gio nodded his unruly black hair and flashed a huge smile once he saw Stella. "For you, Stella, and the group." The word *group* came out like *group-a* in Gio's accent.

Hector hurried to get the door, while Stella cleared a space on Sal's desk as Gio set the tray down.

"Oh. Thanks, Gio," Stella said. "You didn't have to—"

"I heard you say you were...to finish the windows today...so. . ."

"Say, what's this one here?" Hector picked up a tiny dough ball sprinkled with orange zest.

Gio blinked nervously at Stella as if she'd asked. His neck flushed red. Gio blushed almost every time she was around, which was sweet, but. . .

He pinched his thumb and middle finger together, accenting his words. "My nonna's struffoli. Magnifico! The dough, the sugar, the orange, the lemon. Like I say, *magnifico!*"

"Sounds delicious. I didn't know we sold them," Stella said, as both she and Hector plated some. The scent of sugar and coffee drew the others out of the window displays.

"We do not sell. Not yet." Gio nudged his glasses up the bridge of his nose, leaving a flour fingerprint on the lens. Suddenly he cleared his throat and bowed to Stella, one hand over his heart. "I make it *speciale* for you, Signorina Stella." A grin spread across his face.

"Oh. . ." Stella managed a weak smile. *Not again.*

"I'll take one off your hands, Gio, my boy." Alfred butted in, plating some struffoli and a raisin Danish pastry before retreating into Window #1. Billy snatched a handful, popping them in his mouth two at a time. John pushed in between them to pour the coffee into the mugs.

Unlike Stella, the others could think with their bellies. They've never had Gio try to kiss the back of their hand when they returned a stray coffee pot to the bakery kitchen or stood there, mortified, as Gio got down on one knee in front of a crowd of customers and asked her to meet him at the lunch counter down the street after their shifts. (Two women walking nearby had thought it was a marriage proposal and created a whole scene, tearing up and clapping). Stella had felt like a rotten crumb for saying no. But the answer *was* no.

Now, Gio stood there, rocking back on his heels, grinning at her. He was waiting for a reaction. She smiled and bit into one of the struffoli. It was a wonderful zing of lemon and sugar in one bite.

Created speciale for her.

"Mm, good," she mumbled, her mouth full.

It was nice of him. The whole thing, for the group. Breakfast had been the last thing on her mind this morning.

"I think you are going to...not worry...because you make the windows *bellisima*, just like you." Gio's gaze dipped to her waist, then her legs. She hated that he never tried to hide the fact that he was looking at her.

His eyes paused on her hips. "Is a beautiful dress you wear today, Stella. Is a special day, no?"

Oh my God. He's stalling. Waiting for the others to finish up and leave us alone again.

She shot a side glance to Hector, the only one remaining, who stood just a few feet away.

Stella rammed a cherry Danish into her mouth so fast she couldn't respond, only smile with her mouth full.

Of course, Gio would notice her dress today. Hector hadn't said a thing. Instead, he stood off to the side, taking a bite of a cinnamon roll and watching Stella squirm.

"Listen, I'd really appreciate it if you didn't share that the windows aren't quite done yet," she said, changing the subject.

"Ah. Is no *problema*. Your secret is safe with me." Gio winked. "Will you need the lunch, too? I could bring later."

"Well—" she looked at Hector, who offered no help at all. They *would* need food for the group. "It would be a help. I'll grab my purse and—"

"No, no. It will be on the house."

"I insist."

"*I* insist."

She glanced again at Hector, hoping he'd referee, but he only raised an amused eyebrow, which was infuriating.

"Okay, on the house then," she nodded, knowing it would be all the more difficult to turn him down next time. "Thank you."

"Sure."

And then Gio stood there, just waiting for...Stella had no idea what.

"Well, we have to get back to it." She grabbed the nearest box—whether or not she needed whatever was in it—and said a quick, "See you."

She scurried into Window #9.

A minute later, Hector climbed after her.

"So, ol' Gio's still sweet on you?" he said loudly, shoving the last bite of a cinnamon roll into his mouth.

"Shh!" She dropped the box at her feet. "Don't say that!"

"Seems like it to me. Besides, he left a split second after you did."

She cupped her face in her hands. "Oh! He's so nice but he's so awkward. I don't have the heart to brush him off."

"Honestly, I've never seen you more uncomfortable. And that's saying something. I've seen you covered in glue."

She smacked him with the window's sketch then looked around the window that was supposed to be *San-*

ta's Toyshop. A false fireplace had already been set up, and an undecorated silver aluminum tree sat in the corner.

"What? Is being nice really such a bad thing?" Hector leaned against one of the stacks of boxes. "Doesn't Ol' Saint Nick himself endorse niceness at this time of year?"

"It's just that Gio's like a puppy who pees on the floor, then apologizes for it with a smile on his face. He'll invite me to the Woolworth's counter for a malt, and I'll say no, and he'll still smile and be nice to me— which is fine, except he'll wait a week and just ask me again. And again. I don't have the heart to be mean to him."

Hector raised his eyebrows. "I'm still stuck on the first half of that. He's like a *what*?"

"There is such a thing as too nice. For a man."

Hector leaned back, raising an eyebrow. "If a woman doesn't want a nice man, what does she want? I'm curious."

Stella felt her face flush. How was she supposed to answer that?

She glanced down at the sketch. "This woman wants…this window to be done."

"In all seriousness, Gio's 4F, too, for asthma," Hector continued, as Stella ducked down and began unpacking boxes. "You'd think a gal would've snapped him up already based on his age alone. And he bakes."

Hector was right. He and Gio were the only two eligible men under thirty in the entire store.

Which means Hector won't be single for long.

Stella scowled, annoyed with herself. "Let's get to work. This one is *Santa's Workshop*. The tree is up thanks to Joyce yesterday, so we just need to add these toys, a bicycle, and a train set."

"No snowy dwellings that one could drop on someone else?"

"Hector."

"With you, you never know!"

Within five minutes, they'd unpacked the boxes that Joyce had marked with a "#9." Unlike the professional display props that Sal had ordered, this window was filled with toys that Hanover's actually sold and that Stella had hand-picked from Santa's Village: sacks of marbles, dump trucks, a rocking horse, a red wagon, a toddler-sized piano, a 22-inch aluminum model plane (that Hector kept eyeing), dolls and carriages—plus a tricycle and a train set that both needed to be put together.

"I've done train sets before, for Santa's Village," Stella said, sitting down with a Lionel Trains box. "Why don't you take that tricycle?"

"Certainly. I've been known to wield a tool or two, other than a pen, that is." Hector retrieved a wrench from the toolbox and twirled it around like a saber, then joined her on the floor. "Can you imagine growing up with toys like these? My brother and I used sticks for swords."

Stella jutted her chin toward a box of dolls dressed in fine pink dresses and white bonnets. "My mother used to sew dolls for me. I had nothing like those."

She removed the lid from the train set. It was a simple, eight-dollar set that consisted of a black-and-yellow engine, a coal car, two passenger cars, a freight car, and a caboose.

Hector lunged forward. "Wow, would you look at that engine? The detail is unbelievable."

Stella smiled at Hector's sudden giddiness. "Oh, this is nothing compared to the one we have upstairs. It's three times as long."

She got fast to work on the train, spreading out green felt cloth that would be the base of the diorama. This track would be a simple continuous loop compared to the one that ran the length of the fifth floor upstairs. It only took her a few minutes to snap the track together. Then she connected the engine to a series of passenger and freight cars, and finally the caboose. She set up a train station at one end, then opened a 26-piece Happy Farm playset to set up in the middle that just happened to be the same miniature scale.

"How'd you do that so fast?" Hector asked, sitting amid tricycle parts.

She glanced at his thick forearms, noticing for the first time how strong he looked as he held up the bike's handlebars.

"I have the front half done—" He lifted the rear two wheels. "—and the back half. I just need to figure out the middle." He nodded toward the bicycle seat on the floor, a strand of his perfect black hair sliding down over his forehead.

Stella smiled, then glimpsed a vision of Hector sitting just like that on Christmas morning with a child tugging on his shoulder. Just a glimpse. A fleeting glimpse that lasted less than a second.

Her entire body began to flush with heat from her face down. Really? Babies? She never thought about babies, not unless an older woman (usually Eleanor) at the store or old biddies at church asked about a beau and didn't she want a family and blah blah.

Did she even want a baby?

She watched him fiddle with the seat, struggling to find the right screw to hold it on.

Hector's babies would probably have his cleft chin, which would be adorable. *Downright precious*, she thought.

"People with kids..." he said.

"What?" She blushed as if he'd read her mind.

"Parents! How do they put these things together? There aren't any directions in the box!"

"Mm," Stella mumbled. She picked up the plug to the train, handed it to Hector, and nodded at the socket over his shoulder. "There should be an outlet behind you. Pop this in for me?"

"Sure." He ducked behind the Christmas tree, searching for it.

With his back turned, she felt a sudden boldness to ask him about Junie again.

"Speaking of Christmas gifts, is there anything you hope Junie will get you this year?" she said.

What a question. She held her breath, bracing herself for his response.

"There's no spark," Hector said, his head now nearly disappeared behind the Christmas tree.

She sat up straight. "What?"

"The outlet." He poked his head back out, holding the plug up. "There's no power. No spark at all. Can you come look?"

"Oh, sure."

How had he not heard her again?

Losing her nerve, Stella crawled over and took the plug from him, her fingertips brushing his. He leaned back a little as she crawled in next to him by the tree. It wasn't until they were nearly face to face—Stella close enough to smell his last cigarette on him—that she was certain they'd never been this close before.

She ducked her head under the tree and crawled forward a foot or so, feeling the base of the wall for the outlet. As she did, Hector cleared his throat a little. Only then did she realize her rear-end was definitely sticking up in the air toward him. Thank goodness her skirt ended below the knee! She flattened herself onto her belly, her face burning.

Stella hurried the plug into the outlet, then waited for the train to roar to life.

Nothing happened.

"I think you're right, something's—"

Hector crawled under with her, close enough now that his arm brushed hers. "Here, let me." She could smell his Lucky Strikes again. Hector pulled the plug out, wiped it off, and tried it again.

Suddenly they felt too close, lying on the floor of the window almost side-by-side, almost body to body.

"Hmph. Maybe I'm not as good as I thought," she said, hurrying back out. She got to her feet and stuck her head out into the hallway. "Hey, fellas? I plugged the train in and nothing's happening. I think the power issue might be worse than we thought."

John was standing in the corridor unwinding a new spool of wire. The sight of someone else's face felt like a breath of fresh air. A relief. A chaperone even.

"We're still looking at it, Stella," John said. "This is going to take a while to figure out."

The storeroom door squeaked open.

"It's just back this way," a man's voice said.

A familiar voice.

Stella locked eyes with Hector. They both froze.

"Ira," Stella mouthed.

She slid out into the corridor and shooed two delivery boys unloading props in the hall.

"Quick, into the windows! John, go! Take the wiring!"

They gathered up what they could and disappeared inside the nearest windows as Hector slipped out to stand next to her.

Within seconds, the voices grew closer.

"With all the press we've gotten out of our remodel, we're forecasting our best year yet," Ira said. "Our press agent's usually back here if he's not in his office. Checking up on things and what not. Perhaps you'll get to meet him, too."

"Best year, best windows, too, eh?" another male voice responded.

"Darn it, the governor!" Stella whispered. She looked past Hector at a Santa Claus suit—beard and hat strewn across a stack of boxes meant for the animated Santa in Window #6.

She grimaced at Hector, grabbing it and shaking it out.

"Promise me you won't hate me for this!"

"What?" He looked at the suit, wide-eyed.

"If *we* don't have windows, *you* don't have a story to sell the papers." Stella thrust it toward him. "I'd wear it if I could!"

Hector had just finished adjusting the curly white beard when Ira, still dressed in his winter coat and hat, rounded the corner with the red-cheeked Governor Williams, who spotted them climbing out of Window #6.

"Surprise!" Stella stared straight at them, refusing to see how ridiculous Hector looked squeezed into a Santa suit sized for a mannequin.

"Ho! Ho! Ho!" Hector stretched his arms around an imaginary bulging mid-section as the men approached. "Well, I see it's Mr. Hanover and Governor Williams! Have you come to see my work before it's done?"

"Why, yes we have, Santa!" Governor Williams said, taking a sip from a glass he was holding. He wore a tweed suit and a smile as wide as his comb over.

Stella shifted uncomfortably when an exhale of whiskey hit her nose. It wasn't yet 8 a.m.

The governor grinned at Ira, obviously thinking it was a gag planned just for him. "So, you're the one behind all the magic here. I understand your windows are really going to get the people gassed up for the holiday season. Hey, be sure to fill Ira's stocking with a whole lotta greenbacks this year!" He tipped his glass to Santa, then drained it.

Hector issued a completely unbelievable belly laugh. Stella chuckled nervously.

"Ted, this is Stella West. She's our first Head of Holidays," Ira said, giving her a look. She nodded and extended her hand.

The governor shook it. "A pleasure, ma'am." The alcohol on his breath was overwhelming.

"It's 'miss,' actually. Nice to meet you, as well."

"And Sal is...?" Ira peered past Hector, searching the corridor for him.

"Say, governor, how'd you like a personal tour of Santa's Village?" Hector interrupted. "There's no peeking in these windows until this weekend—or you'll find yourself on the naughty list!"

Ira raised a heavy eyebrow, less than amused. "Naughty list?"

Stella held back a cringe with every fiber of her being.

"Oh, shoot!" Governor Williams leaned in and chuckled. "Ira, my wife just may agree with that!"

"Our toy department set records this year," Stella added. "It's been completely transformed for the holidays."

"A tour of the North Pole by Santa himself? I'm in! How's about a stop by that new cocktail lounge afterwards that Ira's been telling me about, too?"

"Now that will keep you warm all winter!" Santa Hector took Governor Williams by the arm, guiding him back toward the door.

"Hey, Ira, get this! Seems I'm being taken up to the North Pole!" the governor called over his shoulder, delighted.

"I'll be along in a minute," Ira called back. He waited a few seconds before turning to Stella. "I'm not sure what you're playing at, Stella, but get Sal's butt in here and finish up."

"Ira, wait! There's something I need to tell you," Stella said, following him through the corridor. "I've been trying to catch you. You see—"

"No excuses!" Ira barked. "The whole season is riding on this. Whatever it is, fix it. Those windows must be perfect by tomorrow morning, or you, Sal, and Santa here will all be out of jobs!"

Before Stella could say anything else, Ira stormed out after Hector and the governor.

Stella pivoted and walked blindly through the corridor, moving like a deflated balloon. Ira had never raised his voice at her, let alone threatened her job.

A window door cracked open.

"Is it okay to come out?" Billy whispered behind her from the door to Window #8. Mina peeked out over his shoulder.

Stella could tell by their worried expressions that they'd heard everything.

"Yeah, fine."

"Should I go back to the truck?" Billy asked.

She wiped her forehead, trying to think clearly. Out of a job? She hadn't been jobless since she was seventeen. Would he really fire Hector, too? This was surely more her fault than his.

"Uh, yes, Billy. Check to see if you have any orders. If not, come back if you can."

Window #7 opened next. Shirley popped out with wide eyes.

"Mr. Hanover sounded angry—" she started.

Stella grabbed Hector's pack of Lucky Strikes from Sal's desk. "Everything's fine." Feeling the tears rise, she ducked her head and walked faster. Then she climbed up inside Window #12, *Heavenly Christmas*, and pulled the door shut behind her.

Stella sat down on the clouds of white puffy cotton that covered the floor, tears blurring out Hector's pack of cigarettes she clutched in her hand. Realizing she didn't have a lighter, she sighed and flopped onto her back.

"Well, you certainly aren't going to finish anything lying down in the clouds."

"Jesus!" Stella jumped. She turned her head to see Ruth, dressed to the nines in a black dress that was perfectly cut to her silhouette, perched on a stool in the corner of the window, sewing wings on angels.

"Sorry." Stella sat up, hurrying to wipe her eyes. "I didn't realize you were here yet. I didn't see you come in."

"I've been here since five-thirty. I'm an early riser." Ruth knotted her thread, then snipped the angel free with scissors. "I had a lot I wanted to get done."

Stella glanced around. *Heavenly Christmas* depicted angels celebrating Christmas up in the heavens. The walls were draped with midnight blue velvet sheets.

Crystal orbs hung from the ceiling, sparkling like stars under the overhead spotlights. A pile of angel dolls with glittering wings lay at Ruth's feet, ready to be strung up next.

Stella got to her feet. "It's really beautiful."

Ruth gave the space a discerning look. "Eh. It's getting there." She dropped the angel into a pile at her feet and regarded Stella. "Now, a question for you. How do you suppose you're going to finish all this by lying down on the job?"

Stella wiped her face. "I'll be okay."

Ruth turned fully toward Stella and took her glasses off. "I heard how Ira spoke to you, and I don't want you to feel bad. Do you know how many people have yelled at me over the years?"

Stella couldn't imagine anyone yelling at Ruth and living to tell the tale. She was certain Ruth could kill a person with her icy blue gaze alone.

Ruth ticked them off on her fingers. "Mothers. Mothers of the bride—more often than the brides themselves. Millionaires. People who act like millionaires. Wives who *think* their husbands are millionaires. Ira, only once, although I'm pretty sure I hollered back..."

Stella cracked a small smile. "I'm fine, I'm just...the store, the windows mean a lot to me. We'll finish, I just don't know how it will all turn out."

For the first time since they'd met, Ruth tilted her head and looked a little sympathetic (just a little).

"That man left you in an impossible situation. If Sal had real nerve, he would've told Ira he was quitting himself. Instead, he took the coward's way out and sent you a telegram." She waved the scissors at Stella. "The way out of tough situations is to fight your way through, darling. Find a way. Make a way. Look at you.

You've assembled a team out of thin air...and you're leading them through with you. The long hours. All these boxes. That's something to be proud of." She put her glasses back on. "The way out is the way through, no matter how sticky." She took up another angel and grabbed her needle and thread. "Now get out there and push through."

Stella wiped her face again. She nodded. Ruth was the best stylist in the store, possibly the best in the entire northeast. "Thanks, Ruth." She glanced around one more time as she stepped to the door. "Your window really is going to turn out lovely."

Ruth turned back to the angel on her lap. "Of course it is, darling. I have a reputation to uphold."

Stella headed back to Window #9, where she threw herself into finishing up *Santa's Workshop*, which she and Hector had started that morning, wondering when he'd return.

Chapter 7

By 11 a.m., Stella had finished setting up most of the North Pole props, had stubbed her toe twice on the same box of oversized candy canes, and was just about to unwrap an oversized polar bear when Billy stuck his head into Window #13.

"Mrs. West?"

This time, she didn't bother to correct him. If she had to pick "married" or "old maid" in the eyes of a high school boy, why not choose the former?

"Yes?"

"I was just upstairs picking up a package for delivery." He scrunched his brow and threw a thumb over his shoulder. "There's a big line forming to see Santa."

She froze. "That doesn't make sense. Santa's Village doesn't open until tomorrow."

"No. Not at Santa's Village. In the hallway on Nine. Outside the bar?"

Stella's jaw dropped.

Hector and the governor.

"Is it a long line?" She dropped the polar bear and climbed out of the window display.

"About ten people with kids, I'd say."

"Oh no, no, no!" Stella pushed past him and bolted out.

The first floor was buzzing with shoppers trying to get a jump on their holiday purchases before the big rush would start the next day. She hurried through Cosmetics. Couples seemed to jump out at her as she passed by. Young ladies Stella's age, giddy at the first signs of the holiday decor, held onto the arms of their men, steering them from one section to the next.

Some girls had it so easy.

Stella had just made it to the top of the first escalator when she spotted Marjorie Hamm coming down the next one. Looking for Ira, no doubt. She didn't have the time or patience for fakery today, so instead of turning at the top and taking the next escalator up, she walked straight into the Women's Dresses department. She busied herself straightening gowns on a rack, buying time so Marjorie would pass.

"Oh, miss!" a refined and velvety voice called. "May I ask your opinion, please?"

Christ on a bike!

Stella spun around to see a woman in her mid-forties wrapped in a full-length chocolate brown fur coat, standing deeper in Dresses, waving her over. Past her, Eleanor was busy chatting up another customer, oblivious to anyone else.

"Yes, ma'am," Stella said, praying this woman only had a quick question so she could get upstairs and save Hector. "How may I help you?"

"My daughter needs a party dress. She's about your age..." The woman sized up the dimensions of Stella's body. "About half a head taller, but just as trim. Something nice. What would you recommend?"

Stella's heart sunk. This was going to take a while.

"Okay." She searched around for the nearest decent option. "Were you looking for a particular style or color?"

"Well, we're having a small soirйe in our home to-morrow night to kick off the holiday season. My husband and I have one every year. Drinks, hors d'oeuvres, piano music...that sort of thing. She'll need something beautiful. You know, something to really get a man's attention."

Stella looked at her for a second as if this was an elaborate prank—a joke the universe was playing on her.

The woman blinked, waiting, as if Stella could produce a magic, man-attracting dress from among the dozens of choices.

"Something to get a man's attention..." Stella walked deeper into the racks. What would get a man's attention? And why on earth did she look like the type of girl who would know? She glanced around, trying to find something that would grab a man's attention without being too tight or too short as to offend a girl's mother.

Oh, hell, she didn't have time for this.

"Well, if I could pick any one here..." She led the woman to the edge of Dresses. "It would be this one." She presented a burnt-gold V-neck satin gown that she'd seen riding the escalator down a few times. It was Stella's own "if" dress. *If* she had time for a love life. *If* she had a beau to take her to a party like this woman was throwing. *If* she would ever get invited to such a thing. It was gorgeous: the V-neck offered just a hint of cleavage without being revealing, the long lantern sleeves puffed at the wrist to balance out the dip of neckline, and the material gathered at the waist to tighten up the waistline. It looked like a silky gown straight out of a Hollywood picture (and expensive at a whopping thirty-five dollars!).

"Yes, this fabric looks lovely," the woman said, running her hand down the material.

"The size is a twenty-eight-inch waist."

"Mm. I think my daughter's a twenty-four."

Of course she is.

"If you need it taken in, they do complimentary alterations on the eighth floor. You could get it altered today."

"That sounds excellent. You're a real lifesaver! I never know what's in style for girls your age."

Stella led the woman over to Eleanor who now stood behind the register. She handed the gown over, happy to pass the customer off to get upstairs. "Eleanor will take care of you from here."

"Mother, have them charge this as well," a voice said from Stella's side.

She pivoted to find herself standing face-to-face with Junie. Hector's Junie. She stood feet away from the counter, dressed in a gray coat with black fur lining around the neck, holding out a lacy cream slip to add to the purchase.

"Ah! My daughter, Junie," the woman gestured toward her. She took the slip without a glance at the price tag and passed it to Eleanor. "Love, this nice clerk helped me find something simply stunning for you." She glanced back at Stella, frowning. "Our poor thing's just had her heart broken and—"

"Junie." Stella blurted out her name like it was an object. *Rock. Boulder. Snowstorm. Avalanche.*

So, it was true. Hector had broken things off.

Stella felt her cheeks flush, and she put her hands up to them as if she could hide them. She wanted to die. Had she really just handed her own "if" dress to Junie's mother, telling her how perfect it would be? And worse, Junie's lacy slip, the kind Stella could never afford or have the curves to fit into, lay on the counter between them.

Stella wondered for a brief second if she could take the dress back and suggest another.

No, that would be rude.

Junie's expression withered a little. "Oh. Hi, Stella." She reached a hand up to pat her perfectly styled golden curls, as though one would dare escape its pin.

"Oh, you two know each other?" the mother said, delighted.

"Mm," Junie responded, looking away.

Stella forced what had to be the worst fake smile in the history of man. She broke into a sweat, feeling like a deer caught in headlights with nowhere to run. She waited for a pit to open up in the floor so she could fall through it.

Eleanor cleared her throat, cutting the awkwardness. "That will be thirty-six fifty with the tax for the dress, and thirteen seventy-six for the slip."

"Oh, Mother, you didn't pick *that* dress for me, did you?" Junie said, eyeing the dress as Eleanor lifted it to wrap it in tissue. Her arms froze mid-air.

"I certainly did. It's lovely!"

"It's dowdy. And the color is drab!"

Dowdy? Drab?

"This young lady loves it." Junie's mother looked to Stella for reinforcement.

She nodded in agreement like an idiot.

Junie crossed her arms and pouted.

Eleanor gave Stella a side glance as if to say, *Get it together.* Her gossip detector was obviously buzzing. Stella could practically read her mind: *Who are these people and why are you acting like a lunatic? Why are you even up here? Why aren't you working on the windows? And why does this stunning girl obviously dislike you?*

"Why don't you try it on, dear?" Eleanor suggested.

That's it. A way out.

"Yes!" Stella perked up. "Eleanor will direct you to the dressing room. I've got to get back to the windows. Happy holidays to you both."

She left before any of them could say another word and zipped up the escalator as fast as she could, her thoughts speeding. Did Hector know Junie was here? Was she here to see him? Had she already seen him? Was he going to this party tomorrow night? Worse, would she really wear Stella's "if" dress to try to win him back?

She could just picture it: Junie waltzing into a fancy dining room looking like Katherine Hepburn in those lantern sleeves, Hector's jaw dropping as he pulled out her chair for her.

The vision made her stomach twist.

As she stepped on the next escalator, Stella wondered if Junie could see it on her face that she knew about the breakup. Could Junie tell that Stella had chosen today's dress, lipstick, and everything with the hope that Hector would notice?

She felt herself begin to sweat through her dress, her Rose Bulgare now just a memory as the escalator chugged up to Six. Why did everything with Hector feel like the stakes were so much higher than with any other man?

Stella stepped off and ran to the bar on Nine, which, in the morning, offered breakfast and Bloody Marys, but Hector wasn't there, nor was there a line. According to Lawrence, the head waiter, Ira, Hector, and the governor had shown up, drained several, then cleared out half an hour ago.

She headed up to the executive offices to find Hector. Ira's door was propped wide open, and his chair was empty.

Cece sat up front at her desk in an urgent conversation on the telephone, but waved Stella over anyway. She slid her a check and a fountain pen, then let the receiver drop for a second and mouthed, "Sal's final check."

No bone in Stella's body could make her sign another four-figure check to that rat. Stella exaggerated a frown and tapped her watch. "Later!" she mouthed, then hurried on before Cece could protest.

She slipped by Ira's office, passed hers, and cracked Hector's door open. She was surprised to find him sitting perfectly upright, squinting through his glasses at the page in his typewriter. Two mugs of coffee sat next to the typewriter, one empty, one full and steaming.

"You're all right?" she said, simultaneously surprised and relieved. "You've been gone for two hours. I thought you'd be three sheets to the wind by now."

"I had Lawrence hold the liquor. I drank at least three tomato juices instead. God, that stuff is awful on its own," he said, curtly, not looking up. "Can't say as much for the governor. Ira had to help him to his hotel."

Taken back a bit that he wasn't daring to look at her, Stella spied the Santa suit tossed on one of the chairs across from his desk. "Thanks for before, distracting them and all. I know you probably felt ridiculous in that getup. Billy ran down and said you had a line of kiddies waiting for you."

A muscle in Hector's jaw twitched as he continued typing, eyes on his typewriter keys.

She closed the door behind her. "That's it? Nothing to say? We could really use your help downstairs if you can. We're starting to make real progress. Ruth's window sure is—"

His hands fell from the typewriter. "I can't. I'm working on a backup press plan for tomorrow."

"A backup plan? You don't think we're going to finish?" She crossed her arms over her chest. "We're getting closer. We're figuring it out."

"That Santa Belle, what's her name, the redhead? I ran into her in the hall. She said Ira threatened both of our jobs if anything went wrong tomorrow. When were you going to tell me?"

Stella's jaw dropped a little. Apparently, the Belles had a gossip chain that rivaled Eleanor's.

"I didn't have a chance. You didn't come back once you were done. I've been working like mad to make progress—"

He leaned back in his chair. "You told me to distract them, so I did."

"I can't believe you've lost faith in this. We will finish, you know that, right?" She put her hands on her hips. He'd never doubted her before.

Hector made a noise that sounded like a grumble as he stared back at the paper in his typewriter. *A grumble.* It tore at Stella's last nerve.

She cocked her head. "Did you just grunt at me? I promise I'm working as fast as I can down there trying to save both our jobs." She picked up the Santa suit and draped it over her arm. "Just forget it. I came to see if you were all right. Obviously, I didn't need to." She headed for the door.

He jumped to his feet. "Wait, don't be cross!"

She paused, her hand on the doorknob, thinking maybe he'd come to his senses. He'd never brushed her off before. He knew what this job meant to her. The last thing she wanted was to affect his work as well.

He smoothed his tie. "You and I still haven't done your training for when you speak to the papers tomorrow. Sal will be a no-show. They'll need to interview you instead. You need to be ready to—"

"You're giving me more work to do? Today?" She spun back, her mouth a little agape. "Just write me notes to read. By the way, I ran into Junie downstairs. She bought a real pretty dress for the party tomorrow night. Stunning, actually."

She watched his reaction, not believing the sass with which the words had come out of her mouth. His lips parted. He shoved his hands in his pockets, looking a little sheepish.

Stella sealed her lips and pushed back out into the hall, heading for the escalator. If she'd needed any kind of nudge to get through the challenge of finishing the window displays, Hector had just given it to her.

Chapter 8

Stella felt shaken as she rode the escalator back down to the first floor. She'd never fought with Hector before, and certainly had never yelled at him. Why shouldn't he go to Junie's party if he wanted to? Not that he said he was going, but still.

She wiped her hands over her face. It was only noon, and she'd somehow already failed the goals she'd set. Instead of telling Ira about Sal, she'd had her job threatened. Instead of finding out what was happening with Hector and Junie, she'd made an ass out of herself in front of Junie and fought with Hector.

And only half of the windows were done, and the group still had serious electrical issues to deal with.

Stella swam back through the lunchtime crowd filling the first floor and slipped through the door into the corridor.

The group, now whittled down to Ruth, Alfred, and a few delivery boys—as Joyce, Luella, and the Santa Belles had gone to start their normal shifts—were eating a tray of sandwiches and lemonade that Gio had dropped off.

Stella was instantly glad she'd missed running into him. The last thing she wanted was another awkward run-in.

Alfred reported that the group managed to finish Windows #10 and #11 and start on #12 and #13 while she was gone. John had run out to try to track down an electrician and grab replacement parts that Hanover's didn't sell.

The small group worked hard and fast through the afternoon. Stella threw herself into decorating like her job depended on it. She dressed the animated Santa Claus figure with the blasted Santa suit that Hector had worn, trying to ignore the familiar aftershave she could faintly smell on it, stopped a tinsel fight among two delivery boys, and shooed a third one away from loafing around in Window #9 with the train set. Naturally, the boys all started behaving perfectly once Mina and Shirley returned during their late afternoon break.

Stella had just started unpacking an all-white manger scene inside Window #14 when she found herself completely lost in thought about her fight with Hector. They never fought. Ever. They only ever had a great time with one another. The best times.

She felt a twinge. Maybe she should apologize. Make everything right again. Normal again. Somehow erase the past few hours from both of their memories.

"Mrs. West?" It was Billy.

"Yes," she sighed.

"There's someone out here to see you."

Stella ducked down and stuck her head out of #13 to see Martin Clark standing behind him. "Darn it!" She looked at her watch, completely forgetting about his 4 p.m. ribbon-cutting run-through.

She climbed back out and dusted glitter off the front of her dress.

"Martin, lovely to see you. I'm so glad you're back this year." She couldn't help but smile around Martin.

He was dressed in a smart gray overcoat, and a black fedora and gloves. His snowy beard was trimmed and tidy as always. He clenched a pipe between his teeth.

"Stella West." He took off his gloves and held out a hand, grabbing hers affectionately, then brushing her cheek. "Don't you look radiant."

Well, that makes Gio and elderly Martin who've noticed, she thought weakly.

"Thank you."

"And in charge of everything this year, I hear."

She nodded. "Mm-hmm. Everything except the parade and the opening moment. That's all Hector's doing."

"Such a brilliant plan. Is Hector around?"

"Yes. Let me call upstairs. He was in his office last I checked."

She'd no sooner picked up the receiver when Hector walked through the door. A little relieved that she didn't have to talk to him without seeing him face-to-face, Stella watched as Hector went straight into his dazzling press agent mode, greeting Martin with a huge grin and leading them both outside.

"The parade steps off at nine-thirty a.m. You're on the final float, which means you should arrive at our front door by ten forty-five," Hector read from the schedule in front of him.

Stella stood there, listening with her arms crossed, slightly annoyed. The walk-through was primarily for Martin, of course, to make sure he felt comfortable, knew all the points to hit, and got all the right remarks down.

Still, Hector hadn't made eye contact with her once since he'd met up with them. She played a part in this too, as her windows would be unveiled as soon as Martin's remarks ended, and the ribbon was cut.

Now, Stella didn't feel like apologizing. Instead, she stood by, smiling politely at Martin, as Hector explained that Martin would step off the Santa Claus parade float right at the parade's finish line. Then he'd join Ira and the governor in front of the store's door to snip the red ribbon and declare Hanover's open for the holiday season. Joyce would then knock on the window to signal one of the guys inside—Stella still needed to decide who—to flip the switch and raise the curtains. Finally, Martin would guide a rush of children and parents into the store and straight upstairs to Santa's Village.

Hector explained where the press would stand, where photographers would be stationed, where he'd hover to give the cue to Martin to snip the ribbon, and whom to hand the scissors to afterwards. They ran through Martin's lines of dialogue three times until it was nearly five-thirty.

"You know, I think you two have planned something just brilliant here," Martin exclaimed, tucking his script under his arm and pulling his gloves on. "This gimmick is an absolute delight! I'm sure the windows will be marvelous as well, Stella. The two of you, your minds together, are brilliant. Ira's got a real dream team with the two of you paired up. This is going to bring joy to a lot of children." He teared up for a second. "And to one old man as well."

Shocked, Stella stepped forward to rub his arm, "Oh, don't—" At the same time, Hector leaned in to offer his handkerchief.

"I'm sorry, I'm sorry," Martin waved them both away. "I'm being ridiculous. It's just that I lost my brother this year."

Stella could see that the sentence still felt new in his mouth.

"He was the younger of the two of us, and a heart attack took him, like that." He retrieved his pipe from his pocket and studied it. "One never really realizes how fast life goes. Not even someone at my age. You go through childhood, then adulthood, then one day you wake up and you find yourself playing Santa Claus. Life goes by so fast that, it really does." He gave them a sad smile.

"The worst part," he continued, "is that we waste so much time being angry at one another, or bitter over the silly squabbles we have. We don't see what's right in front of us. We don't take the opportunities we have to tell someone we love them."

Stella felt herself blush. She pulled her scarf tighter around her neck, dipping her cheeks inside, refusing to sneak a look at Hector.

"I'm sure your brother knew you cared," she said to Martin. "And, well, we sure appreciate you and all you do for the families in this city. You'll bring such joy to them tomorrow."

"Thank you, Stella. And I apologize for getting weepy. 'Tis a special time of year, I suppose. And especially important to share it with the ones you love most while you can." Martin popped the end of the pipe back between his lips. He straightened up. "Well, I best get going if I'm going to make my dinner reservation. I'll see you bright and early right here tomorrow, dressed as you-know-who!"

"Yes, thank you, Martin," Hector said.

"Thank you," Stella mumbled as Martin squeezed her arm. Then he turned and disappeared into the crowd of shoppers on the sidewalk.

She and Hector stood there, not talking for a few seconds. The anger she'd felt toward Hector drained out of her. Martin's words made her feel guilty for being upset, especially at Hector of all people.

She toed a crack in the sidewalk with the tip of her shoe. Should she apologize? Would he? She chewed the inside of her cheek and glanced at him.

"I'll come down and help in a bit, okay?" Hector said. He scratched the back of his neck, looking at her as if asking permission. "I'm waiting on the press bulletin to be delivered now, then I can help with whatever you need."

"Mm-hmm," Stella nodded. Suddenly, the idea of making eye contact with Hector felt like she was choosing to stare into the sun. After hearing Martin's words, things suddenly felt too personal and overwhelming. "All right."

She rushed back inside without waiting for him.

Chapter 9

Stella returned to the corridor to find Joyce, Luella, and Ruth waiting with their coats laid over their arms.

"You three are off, then?" Stella said. All thoughts of Hector fled, replaced with complete anxiety over the ladies leaving. It felt like a huge tick of the clock toward the windows' debut. Stella did a quick calculation in her head. They still had eight full windows to go, not to mention the electrical issue.

"You've gotta see Luella's mural, Miss Stella. It's wonderful!" Mina called from up the corridor, where she stood with Billy and Shirley, who were dishing themselves plates of cold roast beef and potatoes. More rations sent over from Hanover's Bakery.

"I don't want to make a fuss, just wanted you to see it before I'd gone." Luella gave Stella a shy smile, as if she was embarrassed at the attention.

"Well, I can't wait to see it then," Stella said, heading to Window #6. Finally, something else finished! *Take that, Hector Donovan.*

She crawled through, stood up inside, and stepped carefully through the false snow. She backed up as close as she could to the windowpane so she could see it in the way everyone standing outside in the morning would.

"Alfred, flip on light number six!" she heard Joyce say.

The light popped on above her, and for a brief second, Stella could truly imagine herself standing in a snowy forest somewhere in Connecticut. The mural completely wrapped around the entire wall from right to left, flanked with snow-dusted trees. A red barn had been painted in the center, just as planned, with warm light depicted in each of its windows, and smoke piping out of the chimney. A midnight blue night sky was dotted with stars behind it all.

It was beyond lovely. It was perfect.

The only thing missing was the family of animated deer that was supposed to move.

"Oh, Luella, you missed your calling. It's magnificent!" Stella said as she crawled back out. "You should be so proud!"

Luella ducked her head and fiddled with the strap of her handbag with her paint-speckled hands.

Ruth tugged on her fur coat, her gold bracelets rattling. "Yes, yes. Luella must tell her husband all about it. But she won't have a chance to if we miss our ride. Night, Stella. We'll see you in the morning." She gave Stella a curt chin tip before turning for the door, as if to say, *Keep on! The way out is the way through!*

"Bright and early," Stella said, feeling her stomach twist a little.

John returned, just as the trio of women departed for the night.

"Any luck finding an electrician?" Stella asked.

"No." He held up three bags from the hardware store. "Seems everyone's taking a long weekend for the holiday. But I did find a fresh circuit board, a new master switch, and a bunch of other doodads the fella at the hardware store recommended."

Stella massaged the space between her eyes. "Okay. Give it your best. Everything hinges on the figures. Alfred? Can you come help?"

The 6 p.m. store closing came and went. Alfred had switched the victrola from Christmas tunes to up-tempo swing, as he and John sweated over how to fix the electrical issues. A suspicious amount of giggling was coming from Window #16, which Billy and Mina had volunteered to unpack.

Stella was shingling a gingerbread house in Window #19, *A Gingerbread Christmas*, when one of the Delivery Fleet boys stopped in from outside and yelled, "Come have a look outside! It's snowing!"

"Oh! Isn't snow supposed to be good luck?" Mina shouted.

I wish, Stella thought.

"Mina, let's take a break and go look!" Shirley begged.

"Snow's only lucky on Christmas Day," Alfred said. "But heck, I could use a decent smoke."

Stella heard doors open all throughout the corridor as everyone filed outside. She glanced at her watch. She'd been going for hours with only a break for Martin's run-through. She dropped the rest of her cardboard gingerbread men and followed. It wouldn't kill her to take a ten-minute break.

The cold wind whipped as she pushed through the store's front door and stepped outside. The sun had completely set now and had pulled the temperature with it. The streets were nearly empty, except for a few rogue shoppers rushing to their trolleys. Snowflakes had indeed started falling, laying a perfectly thin white sheet over the sidewalk in front of the store.

A few windows over, Billy stood with Mina and Shirley who were twirling in circles and letting the snowflakes fall on their faces. John and Alfred each lit up a cigarette and strolled down toward the clock.

Stella kicked off her heels, which felt like they'd permanently molded themselves to her feet, and stepped her stockinged feet on the ice cold sidewalk. It felt like absolute bliss as the angry blisters succumbed to the icy numbness. As she stood there, shoeless, she noticed a G.I. rounding the corner. He walked with his hands in his pockets and was staring up at the store, moving his jaw rhythmically, chewing gum. She watched him as he paused right in front of Window #10. He stepped up to the edge of the window screen and cupped his hands around his eyes, try to peek inside. When he couldn't see anything, he did the same at Window #9, then #8.

"Strange time for a walk," she said, just as he moved on to Window #6.

His face snapped toward her, as if caught, then nodded at her feet. "Strange time to have no shoes on."

She reddened and hurried her feet back into her shoes.

The G.I. tipped his chin toward the store. "I was hoping ol' Hanover's had their windows up. I ship out tomorrow morning. Back to France. I'm trying to shore up all the nice, shiny holiday memories I can before I go." He pointed back over his shoulder. "Horne's tree is already up. It's swell."

Stella let out a visible breath of air. "Yes, I saw it."

"Not a fan?"

She rubbed her hands together and blew a hot exhale into them, warming them up. "I'm actually in charge of Hanover's windows, so...we're umm, not quite finished yet."

"Ah. The competition, eh?"

When the G.I. didn't move along, she stuck her hand out. "I'm Stella West."

"Private Joseph Harris," he said. "That must be an exciting job, creating windows people love so much."

"Ugh," she said, softly. "It is a good job, but we're having some…challenges."

Just then, Mina let out a shriek from down the street. Billy was chasing her with a piddly snowball he'd scraped together that fell to dust as soon as he tried to throw it at her. He slipped on the sidewalk as he chased her with his cold hand.

"Um, that's my staff," Stella said. "We're taking a bit of a snow break."

"They look fun." He smirked. "Not sure snowball fights would cut it in the army."

"They are fun. But I'm afraid none of us are brilliant when it comes to electricity. We're having wiring issues throughout the whole display."

He removed his hat. "Well, I've repaired an airplane or two in my time. What's the issue?"

"An airplane?" Stella repeated. "A whole airplane?"

His face broke into a grin. "Well, parts of the engine, but that's a pretty important part. Why?"

She couldn't believe her luck.

"We're having an issue with our circuit board and master switch. I don't even really know what that means, but I'm told that's what's happened. Would you be willing to take a look, for an early peek at the windows and all?"

Chapter 10

"Does this guy have any actual experience?" Hector whispered.

He had his arms crossed, staring down at Private Joseph Harris (or Joe, as he'd asked Stella to call him) who was pulling himself into the crawlspace under Window #1 with one very muscular arm.

Instantly annoyed, Stella held back on asking Hector if he was such an electrical genius, why hadn't he crawled under there with tools and wire or whatever else they needed and gotten it done hours ago? Instead, all she said was, "Yes, with airplanes."

Hector frowned. She'd found him waiting for them inside the corridor when they'd returned from their snow slash smoke break, confused as to where everyone had gone to. He seemed ruffled at the sight of Stella returning with a serviceman in tow. His 4F status really was turning into his Achilles' heel.

Joe had introduced himself nice enough. Still, she couldn't blame Hector for feeling a little competition. Joe stood a good four inches taller than Hector and, holy mackerel, in the light of the store, it was impossible to hide how good looking he was. The polar opposite of Cary Grant, Joe was a blonde-haired Ohioan with stunning blue eyes and a jaw so muscular he looked like he cracked raw walnuts for a hobby. He'd sent the Santa Belles into a tizzy when he shed his winter coat, and then his button-down so it wouldn't get dusty in the crawlspace, leaving him in a tight white undershirt that strained over his shoulders and biceps when he stooped down to the floor to investigate.

Everyone had gathered around to see if he could fix their issue. Mina, who had seemingly lost all interest in Billy, was salivating in the doorway with her knee drawn in and heel inched up in a flirtatious pose. Shirley stared over her shoulder, unblinking.

"Adjust the light a little bit?" Joe called.

Alfred scooted closer with the flashlight.

Joe slid out a few seconds later, sat up, and brushed his hands off. "Okay. Stella, you said you had a fresh master switch and circuit board? Your guys have re-placed those well enough, but you're also going to need to replace the wiring under each window, too. That's probably why nothing's working. The wires were prob-ably affected. And you should really do it for safety's sake, anyway."

"Won't that take forever?"

"Well, the new wiring just needs to be hooked up here at the circuit board—" Joe took the spool of wire from Alfred and began unraveling it. The tiny muscles in his forearms flexed with every movement. "—and then someone will need to run the wire through the crawlspace underneath all the windows. We can wire each window so each one has its own power source. That way, if one goes down, the others will stay up."

Stella thought for a second. "I think there's a crawl-space under every few doors, but I'm not even sure if they open."

"You and Mina are probably the only ones small enough to crawl under there. It will be pretty tight. You aren't afraid of spiders, are you?"

"Spiders," Hector scoffed behind her.

"Spiders?!" repeated Mina, whose face went slack as she lost all sense of flirtation and backed away.

Stella took a step forward. "I'll do it." Figuring the way out literally *was* the way through this time, as Ruth had said.

John pulled the dusty crawlspace door under Window #3 open for her. Alfred headed to the next one under Window #6.

She kicked off her shoes, knelt down, and stared into the dark space. It smelled like musty dirt.

"Pass me a light?" At this point, she'd risk dust, dirt, spiders, and ruining another dress to get these figures working. Hector handed her his lighter and she knelt down, then scooted inside on her belly.

She'd crawled halfway in, Hector's lighter in front of her, when the smell hit her—a strong acidic odor that made her eyes water.

"Wait! I think something died in here." She buried her nose into her shoulder and tried to breathe only through her mouth.

"Could be mice. Or rats," Alfred said.

"Rats?!"

Joe flashed his light at her from the head of the tunnel near the master switch. "Here, Stella, get ready to catch this bundle of wire. I'm going to need you to pull the whole thing through. Drop one wire underneath each window. John, Alfred, you can at least fit your arms in and attach them, right?"

They must've nodded, as the next thing Stella knew, the bundle of wires landed at her waist.

"I've got it." She peeled one wire out of the bundle and left it there, then held her breath and crawled underneath Window #5. She spotted something in the brightness of the lighter that looked like piles of shredded cardboard. "Wait, I think I found the smell. I think something's been nesting down here!"

"There's old, chewed wire back here, too," John called from Window #3, back where Stella had crawled in. "There's a four-legged culprit somewhere."

Stella felt a bubble of panic expand in her chest. Hadn't Hector said he'd heard a scratching sound yesterday when they were setting up that window display?

Before she could move, her light caught the reflection of glowing eyes staring at her from deeper underneath the tunnel.

"Something's under here! Pull me out! Pull me out!" Stella kicked her legs trying to back up. A squeak and a hiss darted at her, then turned and scrabbled at her shoe. Something with claws!

"We've got raccoons!" Alfred yelled from above in Window #3.

"Racoons?!" She snapped the lighter shut and threw it toward her feet. Suddenly, a panel pulled away on her right, and an arm shot in.

"Here!" The arm dragged her out from beneath Window #5 as the glowing eyes hissed and lunged at her feet again.

She yanked her legs out of the way just as a piece of cardboard slammed down over the opening, trapping the hissing raccoon inside.

"You okay, Stells-Bells?"

Stella glanced behind her, realizing it was Hector, not Joe, who'd pulled her out. Hector was sitting on the floor, Stella on top of him, sitting pulled back against his chest, one of his arms looped around her waist.

The feel of his arm wrapped so tight around her sent a sizzle up her spine.

"Um…I'm…" she stuttered, shaking.

"There's a whole kit of them in here. And one aggressive mama," Joe said, peering down behind the cardboard. He pointed to Billy and Mina, who'd both huddled in the corner. "Get me a box."

"You all right, Stella? Did it bite you?" Hector said in her ear. Only then did she realize she was still slumped back on his lap.

"No. I'm fine. Thanks."

Stella hurried to her feet and scurried back as Joe pulled out a mama raccoon and three of her babies, kicking and hissing and angry, and lowered them into a box.

Shirley leaned over them. "Mina, look! The babies are cute!" She jumped back when one hissed at her.

There were five total. One mama. Four babies.

"What do we do with them?" Stella asked.

"They need to be released somewhere," Joe said.

Hector peered down over Stella's shoulder. "How about the alley out back?"

"Well, there's a chance they could find their way back," Joe replied.

Stella shook her head. "The babies would freeze to death. And we don't want any shoppers getting bit, especially tomorrow. That would be a nightmare."

"You'll have to release them somewhere a bit woodsy," Joe suggested. "Any place like that nearby?"

Stella waved Billy over.

"I need to borrow your keys."

Chapter 11

"Well, this is one use of a delivery truck that ol' Ira Hanover never foresaw," Hector said, as he slid into the passenger seat of Billy's truck holding the box of raccoons steady. Stella turned the key in the ignition. Thankfully, the engine sputtered to life.

With Stella having pulled the bundle of wire through far enough, Joe, Billy, Alfred, and John had agreed to connect what they could. Stella and Hector would drive the raccoons to the nearest wooded area and release them.

"Just for the love of God, don't let them get loose in here," Stella said, pulling out onto the street, which was empty at this hour, save a few cars coming in the other direction.

"I won't." Hector crossed his arms over the box lid. A furious digging of claws could be heard from within.

Stella let out a long breath. The racoons were a crisis. A miniature, hairy, terrifying-yet-solvable crisis. Just the distraction they both needed to avoid talking about their fight earlier.

She took a corner too fast and bumped the truck's wheel along the sidewalk.

"Hey, watch it! You have driven before, haven't you?"

"What kind of question is that? Have you never been driven by a lady before?"

"No, I'm asking because you take the trolley every day."

"Oh. Yes, I *have* driven before. Just not a truck this big."

"We should've put the raccoons in the back," Hector said a moment later.

"Why didn't we think of that? Where shall we take them anyway?"

"The nearest wooded area is that tiny park over the bridge on the other side of the river. That'll be a good home for them. Should be ten, fifteen minutes there and back as long as there's no traffic."

Stella focused on driving, trying to ignore that her brain was replaying exactly how Hector's arm felt wrapped around her back at the store. What a day it had been, and they still weren't done. She prayed they'd have the electronics up and running by the time they got back.

She pulled to the stoplight in front of Horne's.

"Look. There it is. Taunting us," she said, pointing at Horne's tree shining in the night.

Hector ducked his head, peering through the window. "It *is* bigger than last year. Damn."

"It must be nice to be done early." Stella slid her hands down the steering wheel, waiting for the light to change. "I bet all their employees are probably getting a good night of sleep right now."

"Sleep? What's that?" Hector joked.

The light turned and Stella swerved a bit to give space to a passing truck.

"Hey, careful! My brother's a war hero, remember? For Christ's sake, I don't want to die in a delivery truck full of raccoons. Imagine those headlines!"

Headlines! A dose of normalcy between them. She felt her mood lighten.

"Give it to me," she said.

"Hmm... 'Man and Woman Die in Crash; Remains Eaten by Raccoon Family'?"

Stella cracked a smile. "How about 'Woman Drives Off Bridge After Designer Abandons Her, Ending it All'?"

Hector sat up, enlivened. "No. 'Woman Gets Rabies in Attempt to Finish Hanover's Holiday Windows,' run alongside a companion ad, 'See Santa, Only at Hanover's!'"

"They wouldn't!"

"The Gazette definitely would." He kept on. "For the Post it would be, 'Hanover's Delivers Rabies for Holiday Season.'"

Stella tipped her head back, laughing. "Or 'Racoons Free with Every Purchase.'"

"Say, Ira loves new sales gimmicks! And the Herald..." Hector thought aloud, "'Baby Jesus Saved: Couple Rids City of Window Display-Eating Raccoons.'"

Couple. Her heart flipped. Had he meant to say that? Was he being generic about it? Newspaper headlines said "couple" all the time, right? Stella chewed her lip. But in those cases, they were actual couples, or husbands and wives.

They drove on in silence a few minutes before she snuck a side glance at him. She hated silence between them. Even the damn raccoons had gone quiet.

Say something. Say anything. For God's sake, someone talk.

"Listen, I'm sorry about earlier," she blurted. "I was surprised about you and Junie. I guess I thought you would've told me."

Hector shifted in his seat and looked out the window.

"It's just...the Santa Belles knew and they only just started working here. I've known you forever."

Okay, it was an exaggeration. They'd known each other for two years. But it felt like forever.

He didn't say anything. Why wasn't he talking?

"You won't be single long, I'm sure," Stella said, feeling like she had no control of her mouth. "Half the women in the store are salivating over you."

What was she doing? Why was she suggesting he'd find someone new? The thought of him moving on with someone else—other than her—made her feel...

She chewed her lip.

He looked back at her as they rounded a corner and drove onto the bridge away from downtown. "That's not saying much. Thanks to the war, I'm one of the only unattached men left in the store under the age of seventy."

"Please!" She glanced at him fully this time.

"It's true. Me and Too-Nice Gio, and...who else? Ol' Wilbur in Gloves?"

Stella tried to suppress a smile.

"What?"

"Actually, Wilbur is seventy," she said of the white-haired man who'd worked in Gloves for as long as Stella could remember. "I know because I signed the store's birthday card for him last month."

Hector groaned.

"But you're a catch," Stella admitted. "Such a catch! And with the way you flirt..."

"What? I don't flirt! I'm not a flirt. Are men even called that? A flirt? You're a flirt."

She recoiled.

Hector nodded as if he was dead certain.

"You do flirt," she repeated. "You do that...lean and everything."

"I lean?"

"Yeah. Like Cary Grant in his films."

Hector looked at her blankly.

"He's so tall, he leans over his romantic leads in his films. He leans when he flirts. You do the same thing."

"Who do I flirt with?"

She shriveled behind the steering wheel, sealing her lips shut, not wanting to name names.

Salesgirls. Female shoppers. Santa Belles.

"I don't know names, but you do. I've seen it."

"Well," he crossed his arms atop the box. "I've seen Stella West flirt her fair share as well."

"I do not! I wouldn't even know how!" She passed over the river and steered off into the north side of town.

"Mr. Sergeant what's-his-name can't keep his eyes off of you."

"Who? *Private Joe*? I just met him tonight! He's saving our butts and our jobs. You can't count him."

"You were flirting with him," he mumbled. "You were biting your lip and smiling."

Stella squinted in the dark. Was that flirting in the eyes of a man? She bit her lip when she was deep in thought, but not on purpose—did she? And how could she bite her lip and smile at the same time?

She looked at Hector like he was crazy. "I was being nice to him. For helping."

Hector got quiet. Stella paused the truck at another light, guessing he'd tell her when they'd gone far enough. After turning off the bridge, the road broadened and the wide expanse of a riverside park—a dark patch of grass lined with evergreens and statues—spread out on their right.

"Try up here, near this thicket of trees." He pointed to the side of the road.

Stella pulled the truck over onto the curb, ignoring Hector's groan as she bumped it hard enough to make him jolt in his seat. She turned off the engine and stepped out of the truck. The air smelled like fresh pine on this side of the river. With no maze of city buildings to block the wind, it felt at least ten degrees colder. The snow was piling faster here.

Hector must've read her mind as she walked around his side of the truck. "You cold?"

She nodded, her teeth chattering.

"I'd offer you my coat, but..." he shrugged. They'd both run out of the store without them. "This should make a nice home for them." He set the box down a few feet from the pines and backed away.

They watched the box. It didn't move.

"You left the lid on," Stella whispered, trying to brush the chill off her arms.

"Just...give them a minute."

A little claw poked out of one of the air holes that Hector had made with a key, then disappeared. The box was still again.

"I'll nudge it a little. Maybe the lid will fall off and they'll just go on their own," Stella suggested. She walked a few steps, then stretched one foot out as far as she could and lightly nudged the lid. The lid didn't budge, but something scurried inside.

"Ugh!" Stella squeezed her eyes shut and tried again with more force—too much—and ended up kicking the lid instead of nudging it. The lid popped off, but the box also tipped over, spilling the raccoons out onto the grass. The white around their eyes made them look like little bandits.

But instead of running into the trees, the disoriented mama scurried *toward* Stella.

"Wrong way! Wrong way!" Hector shouted at the raccoon. He crouched down, holding his arms up as if a wrestler was about to spring out of the woods to tackle them.

Stella ran behind him. "Why aren't they scared of us?! Why aren't they running for the trees?!"

"Who knows? Maybe they're city raccoons? Get back!" he yelled.

Stella pivoted and ran for the truck. The mama hissed from behind her, loud enough that she braced herself, ready for a claw scratch or an angry bite at any second. She pulled at the truck's door handle, which didn't budge. Before she realized what she was doing, she hopped up onto the truck's running board, then tried to dive onto the hood, falling short and landing only her upper body. Her legs flailed out behind her, kicking in mid-air.

Behind her, Hector stomped his feet, shouting "Bah!" and clapping his hands, trying to scare the raccoons off.

"Are they gone?" Stella asked, still dangling.

"There, I think that did it—" Hector said, and only then must've turned to see her clinging to the truck's hood. "I'm sorry, what's this?" He laughed his throaty laugh. "Are you climbing the truck to get away from them?"

"No." She broke into laughs too, knowing how absurd she must've looked. "Clearly, I'm *failing* to climb the truck. Is it safe?"

"Yes."

"A little help?"

Stella loosened her grip and slid down just as Hector grabbed her around the waist to steady her.

She was still laughing at herself when she turned to see how close Hector was standing. His face was in shadow, but she could make out the white steam of his breath in the cold. And smell his peppermint chewing gum. And pine aftershave. And starch from his shirt.

It was intoxicating. Not a single part of her dared to move.

She stopped laughing, willingly standing pinned between him and the truck. His hands were still on her hips. He didn't move them.

"I don't lean," he whispered, his exhale hot on her cheek.

Then suddenly, it felt like if he did remove his hands, she'd melt into a puddle of hot candle wax right then and there. A heat she didn't recognize rushed down her spine and moved through her belly, her chest, down her arms to her hands and—

Her hands. Her hands were empty.

"The keys!" she blurted, breaking the spell. "The keys! The keys!"

He jumped back.

"What keys?"

She squinted at the snow at their feet. "Oh no! I must've dropped them when I was running from the raccoon."

Hector stepped back, digging in his pocket. "Blast! My lighter is back at the store."

They both kicked at the snow around the truck, bending over and searching.

"We don't have time to keep looking," Stella said. "We have to get back to the store."

"We'll have to leave the truck here," Hector said. He stepped out into the street. "We'll thumb our way back."

"Hitchhike? From here? Do you think anybody will pass us?"

He shook his head. "Not at this hour. We'll have to walk up to the corner, closer to the bridge."

Stella stepped out onto the road behind him, took three steps, and nearly slipped. She immediately grabbed Hector's forearm to steady herself.

"Sorry! I swear, women's shoes are not built for anything useful!"

"Here, just take my arm." He looped his arm through hers. "Or is this too nice of me? I wouldn't want to go and get a reputation for being *too nice*, now."

"Ha, ha. No. You're not too nice. 'Man Treats Woman Like a Gentleman' would make a fine headline. Besides, old Mrs. McDuffy would be proud."

"Ah, good old McStuffy. I haven't thought of her for a long while."

Things suddenly felt normal again. Any awkwardness had been shaken off by her being a klutz, per the norm.

But Stella didn't want things to go back to normal. She felt...curious. Was it gentlemanly to hold onto a woman's hips like that? Probably not. Had he been joking? Was he trying to prove a point? Or had it meant something more?

And what would've happened if she hadn't dropped the damn keys and sent them both into a tizzy?

She walked alongside him, pretending everything was normal, but inside, the memory of his hands on her hips sent her heart thundering against her ribcage. She gripped his arm a little tighter, wondering if the same feeling by the truck would come back. Perhaps she wanted it to.

They stopped at the corner. The route back over the bridge and into downtown was just a few minutes by car. She felt a spark of hope watching headlights pass by, spaced out by a minute or so. Getting a ride just might be possible.

"Have you ever hitchhiked before?" she asked.

"Not since I was sixteen. And not dressed in a suit, I haven't." Hector turned his head, watching the cross street in all directions. "I'll wave someone down, tell them the truck broke down. We can't very well admit we're two idiots who lost the keys to a delivery truck that we aren't supposed to be driving in the first place."

Minutes passed with no car in sight.

Stella jogged from foot to foot, trying to shake off the cold. Hector, too, began blowing hot breath into his fists to keep his hands warm.

"If this weather keeps up, we'll have a good three inches tomorrow," he said, glancing down at the sidewalk, "Enough to make snowmen." Pronouncing *snowmen* had come out like *SNOWmin*.

Stella was startled.

"What did you say?"

"Maybe kids can make snowmen tomorrow."

SNOWmin again.

"Is that how you say 'snowmen'?"

"What?

"You say it funny. Like it's a last name."

He raised his eyebrows.

"You say it like, 'Mr. Snowmin is here to see you,' or 'I'm having lunch with Mr. Snowmin today.'"

He turned back from the road. "I do not."

"You do too. You just did, twice."

"How do you pronounce it?"

"Snowmen," she laughed. "Say it. Snow...*men.*"

"Snow...men. Better? Stells-Bells, are you difficult to please." Hector pivoted back to the road.

She grinned in the dark, so hard her cheeks pinched. "I will tease you about this forever. You and your good friend, Mr. Snowmin."

"Head's up—" Hector raised his arm, waving. "—one's coming your way..."

He took one step out into the street, waving his hand high. Stella stepped out in front of him and did the same.

Seconds later, a truck sped by with no attempt to stop, driving a little too close and blaring its horn.

Stella jumped back, just as Hector spun her around and pulled her into him, her head tucked under his chin. She squeezed her eyes shut as the truck blew a frosty blast over them both.

She stood there, frozen as the gust died down around them. Her face and the side of her lips were brushing Hector's neck. His fingers laced through hers. Neither of them moved.

Stella couldn't breathe. She felt like every single second they stood there counted—meant something—like their bodies were communicating all on their own.

Then, all at once, the smell of his aftershave, being pressed against him, his fingers wrapped through hers—all of it clouded her.

Without thinking, Stella shifted her face just a little, pressing her lips against his neck, kissing him on the side of his Adam's apple. Her lips lingered there. He didn't push her away. In fact, he didn't move. When she finally pulled back, her cheek brushed his neck, which was now flush with goosebumps.

Oh God, what have I done? What have I—

Hector dropped his chin onto the top of her head, drawing her close. He reached one hand up and cupped the side of her face. Then he dipped his chin around the side of her forehead and kissed her temple, light and soft.

Stella burst into a thousand pieces and whipped away on the wind like snowflakes. Her last boyfriend had done more than just kiss her, but her body had never reacted to a man's touch like this. It felt like sparks were ricocheting through every cell in her body.

Hector lowered his face, making a noise deep in his throat she'd never heard him make before. A soft groan, but lower, more feral. Chills ran up her back. Was this real? Could she actually cause a man to make a noise like that?

Stella dizzily reached up and ran her thumb over the cleft in his chin, just as he looped his arm around her waist and pulled her tighter, pressing her into him from the waist down in a very clear we're-not-just-friends way.

She gasped at the boldness of the move and the want she felt in how strong he held her against him.

"Stella, I—" He paused, lowering his chin, parallel to hers. His lips were so close, she could smell the Lucky Strike on his breath.

Oh my God.

He dropped his forehead onto hers. Her eyes fluttered closed, certain he was going to kiss her. His nose brushed the tip of her nose.

Honk, honk, honk!

A horn and the accompanying headlights made them scatter like kids caught doing something wrong. Stella jumped back, crossing her arms over her chest. Hector straightened his tie for some reason as a black car pulled over. The driver rolled the window down.

"You two having trouble with that truck there? Thought you might need some help."

Stella rode in the backseat feeling like she was in a trance. Their savior, a Presbyterian minister who was returning from a Thanksgiving visit with his sister in Cambridge, Ohio, had pulled over for two people who "looked mighty cold." Hector sat up front next to him, claiming they'd broken down on the way to make a delivery.

Stella didn't hear a word after that. She only replayed Hector's every word, every movement, since they'd set the raccoons loose: she'd kissed Hector's neck and he'd kissed her forehead. And if the darned minister hadn't shown up when he did, what would've happened? What would happen now?

The minister's car paused sharply at a red light.

"Now, that's a mighty joyful sight," he said, pointing out the window. Stella looked up to see the Horne's tree blaring lights at them in the darkness.

She sighed.

Chapter 12

"Jumpin' Jehoshaphat, where have the two of you been?" Alfred said when Stella and Hector finally returned. *White Christmas* was playing for the thousandth time on the victrola. "We were about to send out a search party in case the raccoons had gotten you."

"Oh, you wouldn't believe us if I told you," Stella said, putting her hands to her cheeks, which tingled a bit. Her entire body felt jittery. Hector stepped in behind her, tossing his hat onto the desk.

She wondered if, somehow, any of them could tell what really happened. If they could see it on her face.

"From now on, if we find any creatures of any kind, just put them in Window Six," she said. "They can just live out the rest of their days in *Countryside Christmas*."

"Well, you're right on time," John said, wiping his hands on an oil rag. "We're about to flip the switch."

"You got it wired? All of it? Really?"

"Hallelujah!" Hector stepped up by her side. "Does it work?"

"We're about to find out."

Stella purposely looked away from Hector. She couldn't let herself get distracted. One glimpse of his lips (or his neck, or his hands, or just about anything else) would have her replaying the entire incident, and she needed to focus. Her watch read 10:15 p.m. They had to finish within an hour to get their trolleys home.

Private Joe appeared from behind, still in his white undershirt, wiping grease from his hands onto a rag.

"All right, Stella. We just finished connecting all the circuits, but I'm afraid there's a caveat. Three of the figures, including that Santa in your main window there—"

"Window Six," Hector corrected, taking a protective step toward Stella. She tilted her chin at him ever so slightly, giving him a *shush and please-be-polite* look.

"Window Six," Joe repeated. "Looks like your guy had them brought over from Europe. They have a different style of plug. You'll need adapters to get them going."

"We already checked Hardware twice and couldn't find any," Billy said.

"Don't bother," Stella replied, realizing she'd have to tell Billy about the truck at some point. "Ira donated the entire stock to the war effort. I helped Cece pack them all to ship overseas."

"Then we'll have to telephone an electrician tomorrow," Alfred said. "Or, Stella, we could buy another Santa, one made in America, and swap him in. But either way, the main figure likely won't work for the unveil."

She finally glanced back at Hector. "Is that okay? It will be in all the press shots."

Hector crossed his arms over his chest. "It has to be. I'm not wearing that costume again."

"Someone needs to flip the master switch to see if the rest work. You want to do it, Stella?" John said, waving them all to the main control panel across from Window #1.

"Oh, I don't know." Stella cringed, grabbing the handle.

"Worst-case scenario is that nothing works," Joe said. "Or that we throw a fuse, and everything shorts out."

"Don't tell me that!"

"If that happens, I swear I'll pull the rest of my hair out," Alfred declared.

"Everyone out of the windows!" John called. "We're throwing the electricity!"

Mina and Shirley hurried down the corridor a few seconds later and took a place next to Billy and Hector.

"We're it," they said.

Stella closed her eyes. "Quick, someone say a prayer!"

Billy started reciting the Rosary, but Stella's nerves got the best of her. Without waiting for him to finish, she flipped the switch with a *SNAP!*

The overhead lights dimmed for a second, then stabilized. The sound of tiny gears grinding came to life and echoed down the halls.

Stella gasped. "Did it work?!"

"Sounds like it." Alfred flung open the door to Window #5 then looked back with a huge smile on his face. He gestured for them to peek inside at the tiny penguin figures slowly sliding across the mirror pond on their feet and bellies in the *Polar Christmas* wintery scene. He yanked his celebratory cigar from Santa's Village from his pocket. "All right, that's it. I'm lighting this baby, and no one can tell me otherwise!"

"Huzzah!" John hopped to his feet, lighter in hand.

Joe grinned and tilted his chin up the corridor. "Now you probably want to check that everything is operating correctly. Figures waving or skating in the right direction, animals moving, everything."

Stella ran for the door to Window #9, *Santa's Toyshop*, gleeful at the sight of her train circling the farm playset next to the tricycle Hector had pieced together. The others scattered down the hall checking each window.

"We've got working trains! You did it! Ha-ha!" Stella called.

The Santa Belles squealed at the sight of the moving deer family in Window #6, *A Countryside Christmas*, and again at the dancing gingerbread men in Window #19, *A Gingerbread Christmas*.

We did it. We pushed through, just like Ruth had said, Stella thought.

Joe flashed his smile at her again as he retrieved his shirt from Sal's desk and slipped into it, buttoning up. "Well, now, speaking as someone who's come in from outside of all of this, I think you've done a beautiful job. Very beautiful, if I say so."

"Great," Stella said. "I think we can take it from here. Thank you so much for your help. We couldn't have done it without you."

Stella glanced past Joe at everyone celebrating, but Hector was nowhere to be seen. What was that about?

"Not a worry, miss. I'm just sorry I won't be here to see the grand moment tomorrow." He smiled, shrugging on his brown Army coat. "Must be fun to see all those kids' faces."

"It sure is," she smiled. "Walk you out? I know you have somewhere important to be early tomorrow, too."

Joe said a round of goodbyes to John, Alfred, and the Santa Belles, and shook Billy's hand, who looked starstruck.

Stella paused at the door where Alfred and John were encircled in a halo of sweet-smelling cigar smoke.

"Where's Hector?" she whispered.

"He grabbed his things and headed out," Alfred said in between puffs.

"Headed out as in...went home?"

Alfred shrugged, cigar clenched happily in his teeth.

Stella led Joe back out through the corridor, chewing her lip. It made no sense. Surely Hector wouldn't have gone home without, well, talking about what had happened between them, would he?

Oh no, what if he thinks it was a huge mistake?

She led Joe back out front and glanced at her watch in the streetlight. Eleven o'clock exactly. Minutes to trolley time. She'd have to run for her stop at this point.

Joe paused outside of Window #6 and pulled his hat off.

"Listen, Stella, I wanted to ask if I could see you again when I get back from France. I'd like to get to know you better, if that's okay."

"What?" The question threw her completely. They'd spent only a few hours together, mostly working in the dusty corridor.

Joe stepped closer and grabbed her elbow.

"I said I'd love to see you again once I get back. Would you mind if I call on you? I do know where you work." He smiled.

"Where I work..." Her lips parted, stunned. Was the universe playing tricks on her? The only men interested in her were men *she* wasn't interested in—while the one she wanted had disappeared.

Her mind flipped back to Hector. Had he really gone home without saying a word?

All of a sudden, Joe's face swooped down toward hers. He put one finger underneath her chin and tipped her mouth up toward his.

What the—?

She jerked her neck back and turned her cheek, dodging Joe's lips—just as the store's front door swung open.

"Stel—"

She blinked, having turned her face toward the front door. It was Hector, standing there in the doorway with his coat on, his mouth half-open still stuck on her name, gripping two steaming mugs. She hurried a step back from Joe. So, Hector hadn't gone home—he'd only run up to their offices to grab their coffee cups. She didn't have to ask what was in them. The smell of whiskey and lemon: hot toddies. A celebratory drink for the two of them.

Christ on a bike.

"Umm, I...ahh..." Stella covered her mouth, only then realizing what Hector had seen. Joe had tried to kiss her, and she had been too deep in thought about Hector to see it coming.

Hector stood there looking shocked, then uncomfortable, then something else Stella hadn't seen before.

He must think...he must think...God, what does he think?

"S-s-scuse me," Hector stammered. He rested one of the mugs back on a planter next to the front door, then pivoted and rushed down the sidewalk in the direction of his trolley stop, taking a huge swig from his mug as he stormed away.

Stella backed away from Joe. "I'm sorry, I misunderstood. I can't. I really. I can't." She put her hand on her heart. "But thank you. For the windows. Truly."

Joe nodded. "No problem. I didn't realize the two..."

"Oh, I'm..." Her voice trailed off. *Confused*, she wanted to say.

Joe took a final glance at the boarded-up windows. "Congratulate them for me tomorrow. They're good people." He tilted his head in the direction where Hector had headed. "Might want to check on that one. Maybe I'll see you again."

"Thanks."

Stella took off after Hector, shuffling through the wet snow on the sidewalk.

"Wait!" she yelled once when she'd rounded the clock on the corner, and he was within shouting distance. "Hector! You didn't see what you thought you did!"

But he was already standing at his stop, peering down the street as his trolley approached.

"See, Stella. You do flirt after all. Effectively." He drained his glass. "You gonna be pen pals with him now?"

She recoiled a bit. Jealously was not something she'd seen in him. Ever.

"You don't understand. I thought you'd gone and—"

He raised his eyebrows at her.

"That came out wrong! I thought you'd gone home without saying goodbye and I was confused. I had to thank the man. He's leaving for Europe tomorrow."

It was getting worse. Why was everything coming out wrong?

"Stella, I don't need to know."

Her cheeks reddened. "Don't you think we need to talk about...tonight? Like what happened by the truck?"

Hector's trolley clanged one block up.

He wiped a hand over his face. "It's late, okay? I'll see you in the morning."

"I wasn't flirting, I was being nice. He got the wrong idea," she repeated. "There's a difference between the two."

"'Nice' gets you a lot further than it gets Gio."

She couldn't see his face, and for the first time, she couldn't read his tone.

The trolley pulled up. The door popped open.
He stepped on without looking back. "Night, Stella."

Chapter 13

Stella missed her trolley. She ran for it, even with the brick of stress that was currently sitting at the base of her stomach over this whole kiss-that-wasn't-a-kiss incident. But it was evident by 11:26 and the fresh trolley tracks in the half-inch of fallen snow that it had gone. The nearest place for a gal to catch a safe ride at this hour was the theatre district, which was well-lit and full of people and taxis. Shivering, she turned her freezing feet in that direction and headed off.

As she walked, she ran through the whole nightmare incident in her head. She'd sort of, almost kissed two men in the same night. No, worse. Roughly the same hour. She'd kissed Hector, and Hector was *maybe* about to kiss her on the lips. Joe had darted in for one, but she'd shoved him away. She'd somehow managed to go from no love interest to (almost) smooching two different men.

Oh god, what if Hector thought they'd kissed before he'd walked outside? What if he never spoke to her again?

New headline: Gal Pal Revealed as Mary Magdalene in Time for Christmas; Ruins All Chance at Sought-After Mistletoe Hijinx.

Ugh. The thought alone made her want to go to church and get blessed even though at least half of this wasn't her fault.

How would Ruth's motto, "The way out is the way through!" apply in this scenario? she thought. *What the heck is the way through? How does one deal with a coworker-turned-best friend-turned confusing-I-don't-know-what?*

If there was a way, Stella sure couldn't see it.

After four blocks, she shivered into the theatre district with its glowing marquees and flashing lights. The first performance of this year's "Nutcracker" had just let out, and people were everywhere. Steaming taxis moved up and down the street in slow motion, picking up couples.

Six dollars and thirty minutes later, Stella unlocked her apartment door and slipped inside. She kicked off her shoes. Her blisters were nearly bleeding after such a long day.

A funny light was cast across the living room floor, where her dad was snoring from his armchair, which of course, reminded her of riding Ol' Tillie with him and Hector the day they'd brought it home. Her heart fluttered a little. It was almost like a part of Hector was in the room with her, even though he was in his apartment on the other side of town. Apparently angry and probably really drunk by now.

She peeked into the room to see that her dad had set up their tiny tabletop Christmas tree. It had a handful of ornaments, mostly hand-sewn by Stella's mother years ago, and one strand of lights.

Stella stepped up to the tree, plucked one white angel ornament that her mother had sewn, and held it to her chest. As she walked to her bedroom, she wondered what her mother would've told her about men if she was still here.

Why had it been so easy for her mother? Her mother's family had come to America to open a restaurant. She'd started going to St. Vladimir's Orthodox Church where nuns taught English for free. The church was across from a deli where Dad and his fellow firemen loved to stop. According to him, her mother saw him once and wasted no time introducing herself, even in broken English.

Stella pictured her mother as being so confident—so certain when it came to men. Definitely not a giggly girl, and not a messy, confused klutz either.

She dropped down onto the bed, exhausted. She thought about Ira's threat again. What would she do if she lost her job? Take a semester off of art classes to save money? Pick up sewing and alterations to bring in some cash?

It was all too much.

She took a deep breath, realizing her dress smelled a bit like raccoon poo. *Fantastic.* She pulled it off and tossed it on the floor. Wearing only her slip, she slid underneath the covers, too chilly and exhausted to stand up again.

She stared at the ceiling, running a finger around a loose thread on the ornament and wondering what her mother would tell her to do.

SATURDAY

Chapter 14

"Stella? Are you well?"

"Mm...?" Stella stirred.

"Jesus, Mary, and Joseph, you *are* still here!" Her dad was rapping his knuckles on her door. "Wake up, now!"

Hadn't she just laid down?

She opened her eyes. Her dad stood next to her bed now, dressed in his brass-buttoned, dark blue Class-A fireman uniform.

"What's with the uniform?" She rubbed her forehead. Her thoughts felt all shaken.

"Our truck's in the parade today. Dontcha need to be at the store by now? Thought you'd be in the thick of it already...it's past seven."

Seven. The parade!

She bolted up in bed, wiping her face. "No! No! No! It's morning already?" She'd been so wrapped up in everything last night, she must've forgotten to set her alarm. "I'm late!" She threw back her covers and ran for the bathroom. She glanced at her watch. 7:06 a.m. A full bath would have to wait. She hurried to get washed and brush her teeth.

"D'you want a ride to the parade route?" her dad called from the hall.

"Yes, please!" She ran back to her room, kicked the door closed, and removed her slip. Then she took the dress she'd saved for the big day out of its bag where it hung on the back of her wardrobe door. It wasn't quite her "if" dress, but it was a lovely long-sleeved burgundy one, perfect for the start of the holiday season. She slipped it on and hopped around trying to zip the back.

"I can drop ya at the top of Smithfield. Can you hoof it from there?"

"I'll have to run at this point!" She quickly pinned her hair half-back, then applied fresh lipstick. She started for the hall, then doubled back and dug through her blankets for her mother's hand-sewn angel ornament. She stuffed it in her pocketbook. In the case the windows didn't come off with Ira, she wanted to bring a piece of her mother with her.

Stella glanced in the mirror by her door. This was it. They'd pushed through, and now the time was here. She took a sharp inhale, feeling her pulse start to race. Whatever was going on with Hector was going to have to be put to the side—for a bit anyway.

She raced for the door, then stopped to unplug the Christmas tree. No sense in keeping the lights on if they'd both be out (and it would knock a few cents off their bill).

She shifted the tabletop so she could get behind it and stared down at the funny plug in the socket.

She froze.

"Dad? Where'd you get these lights?"

"Great Uncle Pat brought them over that one Christmas when he came to visit from Ireland."

"And the plug?"

"Had to buy it so they'd work. Probably cost more than the lights!"

No! Could she be this lucky? Stella ducked own. The oddly shaped plug...was an adapter!

"Ha! I need to borrow this, Dad." She yanked the plug from the wall—the lights went dark—then popped off the tiny brown adapter. "Hurry! Let's go!"

Fifteen minutes later, with every second feeling like an agonizing tick of the clock, Ol' Tillie paused long enough for Stella to jump down onto the curb. She threw a wave to her dad in the passenger seat, who responded with a smile and a quick twirl of the siren.

She started downhill toward the store, pulling her coat tight and clutching her purse, adapter and angel inside. She could already hear the parade crowd blocks away: the echo of laughter, applause, squeals, the thunder of marching bands echoing off the city buildings.

Her heart began pounding along with the drumbeat. What if they actually pulled this off?

At the end of the block, she could see Billy and a few other Delivery Fleet boys. Billy had seemingly already been driven back to retrieve last night's truck, and now sat atop its roof, craning his neck for a look at the parade.

"Billy!" she shouted. "Get inside!"

He slid down. "What about our deliveries?"

"No truck is going to get through this crowd for at least another hour. We have to finish up! Look!" She held up the adapter and pulled open the store's side door.

Hanover's first floor vibrated with a sense of nervous anticipation. As Stella rushed through, she passed salespeople hurrying to straighten up their displays and unpack last-minute stock. The silver aluminum trees and ornament-dripped garland in Cosmetics seemed to gleam a bit brighter, dressed and ready to welcome holiday shoppers. Ahead, she spotted Marjorie Hamm buzzing about the new Ol'Christmas Cheer station that sat just inside the door and sold fresh-cut Christmas trees bundled in twine for $1.69 and hot chocolate for .25 cents. The scent of both hit her nose as Stella neared Fine Jewelry, where Gio and a handful of other members of the bakery team were waving a group of college-aged Christmas carolers back away from the store's front doors with a promise of free coffee and pastries.

Maybe he is just a nice guy after all, Stella thought.

A charity bell ringer stood just inside the door with his bucket and bell, ready to step outside and set up the moment the parade ended.

There was no sign of Hector, but that was to be expected. He'd be out shepherding the pressmen and photographers into position or keeping Ira's nerves tempered.

Stella rushed Billy inside the corridor, where the victrola was already playing. John and Alfred were securing the overhead lighting in each window.

"Gentlemen, I have it! I've got one!" Stella announced, holding up the adapter. "Is it the size we need for Santa Claus?"

"Might be! Where'd you get it?" Alfred asked, hurrying through his keyring for the key to Window #6.

"My own home!" Stella pointed at Billy. "Go! Make sure all window access doors are closed."

Billy nodded and ran through the hall.

Stella rubbed her freezing hands together as she watched Alfred lean into Window #6 to plug in Santa.

The crowd outside began clapping along as a marching band passed by playing "When the Saints Go Marching In." According to the parade rundown, which

Stella had memorized by heart, the song was being performed by Peabody High School's marching band, the second-to-last band in the parade. The moment was almost here.

"Did it work?" she asked.

Alfred slid out a few moments later. "It fits! Hit the power for Six!"

Stella stepped to the main control panel and flipped the master switch, then ran back to #6, squeezing her head in next to Alfred's.

Santa shuddered to life, bending at the waist and waving one arm.

"Oh, it's a miracle!" she clapped.

"Well, I'll be damned," John said behind her.

"I have to give it to you, Stella," Alfred said as he dusted his hands off, snapping the door shut. "You did it."

"We all did it. Besides, we still need two more for penguins, but they're on the other side of the store. We can worry about figuring out a fix for them later."

Just then, Joyce popped her head into the corridor. "Stella, you're here! Hector's looking for you. It's almost time."

Hector?

Butterflies jolted up from Stella's belly and went straight into her head.

"Yes! All right! Everyone out of the windows." She wiped her forehead. When had she started sweating? "Only John stays back to open the curtains at Joyce's signal. Everyone else can watch from outside."

Stella ran back to Window #12, *A Heavenly Christmas,* adding one last touch to Ruth's window as Alfred switched off the victrola.

John stepped up to the master switch, hands behind his back, waiting.

"Don't throw it until you hear Joyce's signal!" Stella reminded him.

Then she ran out the door.

Chapter 15

Stella bumped open the store's door with her hip and stepped out behind a wall of spectators cheering as a clown car pulled up. All along the parade route, people stood nearly elbow to elbow. Children were held up in their parents' arms or sitting on their fathers' shoulders to see. Across the street, people peeped out of second-, third-, and fourth-floor windows down at the parade. One man had pulled a chair up onto the roof of his building and sat there bundled in his winter coat.

Stella nodded to Joyce, who stepped to the far end of Window #6, ready to give the signal.

She continued on, squeezing through the crowd, searching for Hector. She couldn't wait to tell him Santa was moving. She'd fixed the window in time for the pictures.

A little girl with braids shrieked and pointed as a sailor balloon floated into view a few blocks down. This was nearly it, the last balloon in the procession. Behind it would be Brentwood High School's marching band, and then Martin (dressed as Santa Claus) sitting in his sled and reindeer float.

Stella wriggled around two large families toward the press riser. Pressmen occupied the first two rows, and photographers took over the middle two, snapping away. Ira and the other store executives stood at the top.

"Stella!" a woman's voice called from behind the riser.

Eleanor was waving at her and juggling a fussy grand-baby on her hip.

"I just wanted to say how odd that mother and daughter were yesterday!" she shouted over the noise. "Would you believe they didn't end up buying that dress after all that fuss?"

Stella paused. She'd almost forgotten that whole interaction with Junie and her mother.

"And the girl said something strange about her former beau," Eleanor continued. "Said he was in love with someone else, someone he worked with? Then she declared she never wanted to shop at Hanover's again."

Stella's heart felt like it plummeted straight through her body and onto the pavement below.

"She said that? In front of you?" she asked. "You're sure that's what she said?"

"Yes! It was so odd. But she's a friend of yours, right? Do you know what she was talking about?"

Stella chewed her lip. She'd struggled to tell Hector how she'd felt about him because she was afraid he wouldn't feel the same, and then she'd lose him. Work wouldn't be the same. *Life* wouldn't be the same if they lost one another.

What if Hector felt the same way? That would explain why he'd been so slow to tell her about Junie.

And Hector, maybe, *loved* her?

She felt a rush of joy cloud her head. All at once, Stella pulled a very surprised Eleanor and her fussy grandson into a hug. "I don't know, but I'll find out. Merry Christmas, Eleanor!"

Without another word, she rushed away and scanned the press section for Hector.

He found her first.

"Stella! Hey, Stella!" He was leaning down from the side of the risers, waving at her. He was dressed in his best suit and wearing a new black fedora, the one she'd suggested in passing weeks ago. A sprig of holly was pinned on his lapel.

Chills washed all over her at once. Everything about him suddenly looked brand new. His smile, the cleft in his chin, the way he towered over most people. Heck, he was more handsome than Cary Grant because he was real and right there in front of her.

She smiled.

"Hector, it works! We got Santa to—" Stella shouted, but stopped short. Hector's brow was creased, and he was frowning.

"What's wrong?"

He threw a thumb back over his shoulder, motioning at something behind him, and waved her up.

"Get in here, quick!"

She squeezed through the pressmen. Next to Hector stood Governor Williams with his ridiculous comb over and his mink-wrapped wife. Beside them was Ira and his wife, Grace Hanover, surrounded by a trio of reporters.

Hector reached an arm through, hoisting Stella up— but as he did, she saw exactly what had upset him.

Sal Sullivan.

Sal Sullivan: deserter of window displays.

He was standing next to Ira, humoring the press, waving a cigar and gesturing back toward the store.

"He's taking credit for everything, Stella," Hector whispered in her ear, his grip tight on her arm. "Bastard just reappeared here this morning. Apparently, Paris and the mistress didn't work out."

Stella's face flushed, thinking of Luella's mural, Ruth's angel display, the Santa Belles, the delivery boys, Private Joe, the Goddamned raccoons. Not to mention the unpacking and stringing and hanging and sore thumbs and toe blisters and late nights and no sleep.

"But he can't...he can't do that...he did *nothing*. He ran out! I swear I'll—"

"Stella," Hector grabbed her by both arms and spoke into her ear. "I saw him as soon as I got here. I ran upstairs and had these printed." He held up a stack of press bulletins. "I'm a press agent by heart, but I have to do what's right. Sal was a good story—"

"Hector, no. You can't!"

"Stells-Bells, I need you to listen to me. This bulletin is better."

"What does it say?"

Hector let out a shaky breath. "I also revised your talking points."

"What do *they* say? I can't endorse that man! I won't!" She took the copy he handed her.

Just then, Ira spotted her.

"Stella, good morning! Good to have you here. It looks like it's almost time!" Ira pointed past them, just as Brentwood's marching band started up "White Christmas" and Santa's sleigh pulled into view blocks down.

"You have no reason to doubt me." Hector curled his hand around hers for a split second, then stepped back, nudging her toward Ira and Sal. "Go!"

Hector climbed down to the pressmen below, passing out the revised bulletin.

Numbly, Stella nodded hello to Grace Hanover, who naturally looked like a million bucks in a floor-length honey-colored fur coat, a diamond snowflake lapel pin, and a cream hat. Stella shuffled around her, following Ira over to the reporters who crowded around Sal.

"—and that's really where the inspiration came from," Sal yapped. "Especially the animated figures, they…"

Ira nudged Stella into the conversation.

"Gentlemen, I'd like you to meet Stella West. She's the brains of the operation. Our Head of Holidays."

Stella refused to look at Sal, gritting her teeth and feeling the Ukrainian in her blood curdle.

Trust Hector. Don't go Stells-Bells on Sal.

She clutched Hector's paper and focused on it instead.

Ira continued. "This bright gal's over all the holiday decor in the store. All twelve floors of it!"

A few flashbulbs went off in her direction. Sal's elbow brushed hers as he angled himself into the frame. He smelled like body odor and beer.

If a human could erupt into fire, Stella would've right there.

She leaned back. "Ira, may I please have a word? In private?"

"Nothing wrong, is there Stella?" he said through his smile as more flashbulbs went off. "I thought I made that clear yesterday."

"Stella! The talking points!" Hector barked from the crowd before her feet. Ruth, Luella, the Santa Belles, and Billy had gathered in front of them now, too.

She caught a glimpse of Ruth's face in the crowd, who nodded curtly to her.

Stella nodded back, ever so slightly.

"Yes, let's hear a bit from Ms. West," a newspaperman asked, tapping his notepad. "What can you tell us about the windows this year?"

"Well—" she peered down at Hector.

"Trust me," he mouthed.

She swallowed. She trusted him more than anyone.

Stella glanced down at the page.

"I have a statement here." She brushed a strand of hair behind her ear and began to read. "This year's theme, of course, is 'Home for the Holidays.' For many members of this city, there are loved ones missing from their celebrations this year—fathers, brothers, sons. Loved ones who are bravely fighting for the safety of the United States of America and for the good of freedom. 'Home for the Holidays' is a series of windows that let passersby peer into celebrations of our blessed holiday around the world, from right here in the city, to the North Pole, to heaven up above."

Some claps arose from those crowded around the pressmen, who were busy taking notes.

She glanced at Hector, who was keeping an eye on Santa's approach. He drew a circle in the air with his finger, his signal to wrap it up.

"As part of this theme, Hanover's, for the very first time, pulled on the talents of...of those working in the store to bring the windows to life." The crowd one block over cheered as Santa neared. "Like many in the city, Hanover's touches the heart of so many who work here that they consider it their second home. For some, we are each other's family, and Hanover's, a second home." She paused long enough to meet Hector's gaze. "A special family full of people who love this store and love serving customers during the holiday season. For us, as well as you, the holidays wouldn't be the same without Hanover's windows. So, this year, Hanover's employees have served for hours to ensure our windows would be more beautiful than ever before."

Stella felt her chest swell from Hector's words. She glanced down at him, catching the quickest smile pass his lips before he turned serious again.

He was right, as usual. It was a good story.

One of the newspapermen waved his pencil in the air. "Ira, I'm confused. I thought these were Sal Sullivan designer windows."

Hector climbed up in between Ira and Stella. "Sal set everything in motion, but as time went on, it was clear that adding the true heart of the store—its employees—into the windows was—"

Stella felt Hector touch her back at the word *heart*. All breath left her, and she felt as light as a feather.

"—the right thing to do this year," Hector finished. "Now, gentlemen, I think this is the moment we've all been waiting for."

Hector pointed down the street just as the Santa Claus sleigh float pulled up to their block. Cheers rippled through the crowd around them. Literally on cue, white confetti began to fall, tossed down by Hanover's employees from the roof. Martin stood and waved.

Hector jumped into action. "Ira? Governor? It's time. We need you in position at the front doors."

Ira's face was red, suppressing confusion and anger for the sake of the press.

Hector led them to the door, leaving Stella on the bleachers with Sal, who silently rocked back and forth on his heels. All his braggadocio had deflated like a week-old balloon.

"Listen, Stel, I—" he started.

All the anger drained out of her. She rolled up the message points Hector had written and gripped them tighter. She didn't want to feel anything but *everything* she felt for Hector. The overwhelming urge to tell him exactly how she felt washed over her. She had to tell him for real this time, without waiting for *him* to tell her first. No more guessing games. There wasn't time, like Martin had said. And people like Mrs. McDuffy can stuff their old rules about manners and men and women in love and courting. The world had been upended by war and all the rules had changed. As far as Stella cared, McDuffy and the rest of the world could go kick rocks.

She scrambled down, leaving Sal behind. She caught glimpses of Hector guiding the governor and Ira over to Santa through the crowd. Cece had recruited two delivery boys to stretch a shiny red ribbon across the front doors. Joyce still stood at the corner of Window #6, waiting to give the signal.

Stella pushed to the edge, standing behind one of the delivery boys.

"Ho, ho, ho!" Martin shouted. "Thank you, Mr. Hanover, for welcoming me back to the city for another beautiful Christmas season. I can't wait to welcome all of you—" He turned to the crowd. "—into my beautiful village, where all Christmas dreams can come true."

Children shrieked and giggled. One boy wearing green mittens stamped his feet.

"That's right, Santa," Ira said, having memorized the script Hector had written for him. Cece handed the governor an oversized pair of scissors. "Thank you, ladies and gentlemen, for being here to celebrate the start of the holiday season with us today. Hanover's Department Store windows have been a time-honored tradition for this city since, well, since I was a boy, and my grandfather ran the place. Like so many of you, I grew up having a cherished place on the sidewalk for these happy moments. I'm pleased to say that this year's windows are the best yet."

Stella's heart pounded, her confidence flickering just a touch, hoping to God that Santa would still be waving when the curtains were pulled back.

"Well, it's about time to officially dedicate the windows, isn't it, Mr. Hanover?" Martin asked.

"It sure is, Santa. Governor Williams, can I get some help?"

The governor took the scissors as Ira stepped back. "I have to say, Santa, I was excited to be a part of all this today, and boy, has it delivered. But learning that the employees in this store put these glittering displays together with their own hands, well—" He pointed at Ira. "—that just goes to show what kind of heart a place like this store has. Can we get a round of applause for Hanover's?"

The crowd clapped again.

Hector finally glanced away from the governor and caught Stella's eyes for just a second. She knew he was happy. After all they'd been through, it was going flawlessly—for the spectators anyway.

She was so happy, she could melt.

After the ribbon fell, Stella knew it would be sheer chaos. The crowd was going to rush the windows and the store to get upstairs to Santa's Village. Hector would be managing the press for hours afterward. Stella would need to handle any issues that came up at Santa's Village, and ensure the windows stayed up and running until they finally turned them off at 10 p.m.

Still, she couldn't wait any longer. She had to tell him.

As the governor opened the scissors and posed for a few pictures with Ira and Santa, Stella flipped open her pocketbook and rummaged for a pen. She turned over Hector's talking points and scribbled a message on the back, then folded the note in half.

Martin stepped to the center of the ribbon.

"Ho, ho, ho! Now, Mr. Hanover, I think it's time to let all these little youngsters up to my village to explore the wonders I have for them straight from my workshop. I can't wait to hear their Christmas wishes this year."

"Sounds great, Santa."

"Ready on three!" Hector directed.

Time to work. Focus!

Stella stepped behind the end of the ribbon near Joyce.

The crowd counted, their excitement drowning out Santa and the shouting of Governor Williams.

THREE! TWO! ONE!

Ira and the governor snipped the ribbon and it fluttered to the ground.

Martin threw his arms in the air. "I declare the Christmas season has begun!"

Stella nodded to Joyce, who knocked on the window.

All along the sidewalk, it happened. The curtains raised at once. The polar bears rocked, the penguins slid, the winter gnomes tipped their hats, the gingerbread men danced. And Santa waved to everyone from inside Window #6. Flashbulbs popped. The photographers went crazy seconds before the crowd pushed in.

Stella could hardly believe her own eyes. Somehow, by some small chance, they'd found a way to pull it off, finishing twenty-six windows, despite all odds.

The way out was the way through.

There were oohs and aahs, then a scattering of applause from the crowd seconds before everyone rushed forward for a better look.

Then the front doors of the store flung open, and Martin waved for families to follow him inside.

"Hector!" Stella shouted, doing her best to squeeze through the chaos—the note she'd written clutched in her hand.

A wave of shoppers practically pushed her into the store. Ira and Hector stood just inside, before the Ol'Christmas Cheer station. Ira beckoned her over, furious.

"Stella, a word. What is this about the windows? Why drop Sal at the last minute? Those papers called me a fool earlier this year. Now the two of you made me look like one in front of the press!"

"You don't understand, sir. I tried to tell you, but between Thanksgiving and your schedule—"

"Sal's a pro!"

Hector stepped forward. "Sal's a drunk who ran out on you, sir. And the store. And Stella."

"It's true," Stella said. "He sent us a telegram on Thanksgiving. We had no warning."

"Oh, darling," a female voice cooed. "You didn't look foolish at all. In fact, I think the idea is marvelous."

Stella turned to see Ira's wife cutting through the crowd toward them.

"Stella, dear, it's a real heart-tugger. Congratulations." Grace leaned in and gave her a kiss on each cheek. "I only saw two so far before the crowd nearly trampled me, but I can tell they're exquisite."

"Thank you," Stella said, then turned back to Ira. "I've been leaving messages with Cece since I found out. We did the best we could with what we had. I promise you." She gripped and regripped her note to Hector. It would be amazing if they didn't get fired. The icing on the cake after how well the unveil had gone.

"I think they turned out wonderful," Stella added.

"She's being modest, dear," Grace said. "And her remarks were perfect. Stella, you made Hanover's sound full of heart, which is what the city needs in a war year!"

Ira dipped his head, submitting. "You really like it, Gracie?"

Grace swept forward and took him by the arm. "Absolutely. It's not so commercial like the other stores, dare I say. You really do have some talented employees."

Ira nodded silently, thinking it over. Stella exchanged a glance with Hector, who was holding his breath.

"All right, you two. We'll talk about this more on Monday."

Monday? Monday! Stella released a huge exhale. It meant there was a Monday in store for the both of them. They weren't fired.

Stella held back a smile as Grace guided Ira away, cooing over the first-floor decorations as they walked.

Cece squeezed past next, hair disheveled and glasses askew, still holding the giant prop scissors under her arm. "Hector! The press brunch!"

Hector turned to Stella, but she planted the note in his hand before he could say a word.

"What's this?" he mouthed as he walked away.

"Just read it!"

Her heart pounded against her ribs. There was no going back now. No matter what lay at the end, she was on her way to finding out.

Chapter 16

After hours of calling *real* electricians to come and run a safety check on the windows' lighting and securing a dozen more electrical adapters (from Woolworth's of all places), Stella took one last lap through Santa's Village. The crowd had settled into a regular twenty-five-min-ute-long line of children waiting to see Santa and an even longer line at the cash registers.

She checked her watch, slipped out of the chaos, and headed up to her office. She stopped by Cece's desk and pulled out a handful of checks, making one out carefully to each employee who had helped with the windows, smiling as she made one out to Billy and the other De-livery Fleet boys. Seven dollars in one check would be more than some of them made in a month. (She slipped an extra five-dollar bill of her own into Billy's check as a thank you for retrieving the delivery truck for her).

Stella grabbed her keys and pocketbook and headed down the maze of escalators, the store still lively with shoppers on each floor. Outside, she turned right on the sidewalk. A family stood dressed in winter coats and hats, including two little boys with hands pressed to Window #5, *Polar Christmas.*

"Are those real penguins, Mommy?" she heard one say.

"No, dummy! They're puppets," the older boy said.

The first one ignored him, pleading, "Mommy, can Santa bring me a penguin for Christmas?"

Stella continued through the crowd, trying to plan out exactly what she was going to say to Hector. Tell him again he was wrong about what he'd seen last night? Apologize for pushing about Junie?

No, don't talk about Junie. Don't bring her up at all. Or Joe. This is about you and him. When he gets here, just tell him...tell him...

She held her breath as Hanover's clock on the corner came into view.

Tell him how you feel.

The arms of its face read 9:55 p.m. He was supposed to meet her at ten.

As she walked, insecurities wrapped around her like the cold. What if he didn't show? What would she do then? Just pretend the note was some kind of gag and forget it? Move on with her life?

No. Eleanor had told her she'd overheard Junie and her mother talking. *He was in love with someone else.* If that was true...if he loved her...

She rounded the corner. She needed a minute to think.

But Hector was already standing there, waiting.

She skidded to a stop. She hadn't anticipated him beating her there.

"Well, now. Isn't this a chance meeting? You see, I'm to meet a..." He held up the note, squinting at it. "...a Mr. Snowmin here."

Stella pursed her lips, trying not to laugh, then felt her entire face blush. She was standing with Hector underneath the clock. The clock where families met. Where lovers kissed hello and goodbye. Any words she'd somewhat planned to say jumbled in her head.

"I asked you to meet me here because...I...I didn't kiss Private Joe. I mean, he didn't kiss me. We didn't kiss. I didn't let him," she blurted.

Hector opened his mouth to speak, but Stella beat him to it. It all flooded out, inarticulate and rushed and very un-quoteworthy.

"He tried, but I didn't notice. I didn't notice at all because all I could think about...was you. And us. In the woods." She dipped her eyes. His brown eyes felt like searchlights, looking straight through her, reading her thoughts. "And how you make me feel every time I'm with you. I was so deep in thought I didn't hear a single word he was saying. But what you think you saw...you didn't."

Hector took a step closer. Everything around them went muted and blurry like a shaken snow globe. They were now close enough to touch.

"Stella, I understand. And I'm sorry I got heated last night." He tipped his face down toward her. "I didn't tell you about Junie because I didn't know what to say. Or what to do because I—" His voice trailed off. "Junie was easy. Wait, no, I don't mean...not easy like that. She was easy to be with because she was everything I was always told to look for in a girl. She's pretty and nice and goes to church on Sundays and comes from a swell family. A rich family. Her parents like me. Even their dog likes me. But she's...easy."

Stella raised her eyebrows.

"With her, I knew exactly what to expect," he continued, "but I don't want something easy. I want...adventure. That's what you are to me, Stella. A messy, wonderful, never-gonna-guess-what-happens-next, riotous adventure." His mouth moved into his half-smile. "In the past seventy-two hours, I've tackled raccoons, trod through a forest, hitchhiked, wore a ridiculous Santa getup—all because you asked me to. And somehow you still managed to finish all of this."

He slid a hand around her waist and dropped his forehead to hers. "I act crazy when I'm with you, because I'm crazy about you." He lowered his voice. "You are a messy, clumsy, wonderful, beautiful adventure. You are not easy. You're what I want."

Stella couldn't move. Her feet felt glued to the sidewalk.

"You're leaning..." she mumbled.

He tipped his chin down toward her and nodded. "I *am*...leaning."

It was the most sensual thing a man had ever said to her.

Before she knew what she was doing, Stella pushed up onto her toes and pressed her lips against his. It was light at first, the sensation of lips meeting lips for the first time.

Hector's lips!

Chills rushed up the back of Stella's spine.

Then Hector cupped her face in his hands. Stella took a step forward, pressing up against him, and suddenly, they were kissing each other deeper, faster—as if neither one of them wanted to stop. He made that same low, feral groan deep in his throat that he'd made back in the woods. Hearing it was fuel to her fire. Stella's entire body flushed. Her winter coat felt stifling.

"Youth these days! Vile if you ask me!"

The snappy voice of an old lady broke their spell. They parted, but this time, without scattering like they had the night before. Hector's face was flushed, his ears red. He paid no mind to the old lady, smiling down at Stella. He narrowed his eyes.

"Headline for you?" she offered.

His half-smile was back. "Give it to me."

"'Girl Meets Boy'..."

"Mm...I've heard that before. Not good enough."

"'Girl and Boy Fall in Love'."

"Love? Gee whiz," he whistled. "More."

She wrapped her arms around his waist. "'Girl Falls in Love with Boy; The Two Never Part Again.'"

"That one's not bad, but—" Hector started, but Stella had interrupted him with another kiss. They stood there kissing, until Stella felt very aware of how many layers of clothing they had on between the two of them.

And how badly she wanted that to change.

The lights in Hanover's windows suddenly went dark. Stella pulled back. She squinted up at the clock. Ten twenty.

But Hector stared only at her. "Stella West, I am officially reporting that you *are* biting your lip."

"Darn it!" she realized, relaxing her mouth into a smile.

"I don't want to say goodnight."

Hector had blurted exactly what Stella was thinking. She ran her thumb down his jawline and over the cleft in his chin.

"Then let's go," she whispered.

"Go?"

"Home." She nodded back toward the windows. "I've seen twenty-six ways to spend the holidays. But there's only one home I want to go to."

He raised his eyebrows, unsure.

She nodded. Together as a couple or not, they'd known each other two years. Leaning up on her toes again, trembling, she whispered, "'Woman Spends Night, Has Fantastic Time.'"

Hector practically knocked her over jumping off the curb to hail a cab.

"Taxi!"

One immediately peeled to the curb, as though the driver and Hector had made a deal in advance.

She glanced back at the window for *A Heavenly Christmas*, where just before the unveiling, she'd added her mother's hand-sewn angel in among Ruth's finely crafted ones. Her mother never had the time to talk to her about men, but the one lesson she did teach her in their short time together was that life was too short. (Hadn't even Martin agreed?).

Stella wanted to stop waiting and feel alive. Now.

She stepped off the curb toward Hector, who was holding the taxi door.

"'Has Fantastic Time,' huh?" He raised his eyebrows as she stepped up to get in. Then he leaned down, murmuring, "I think that might just have to be a multi-part series."

"Please..." Stella said, taking a seat, simultaneously shaking and feeling like she was somehow glowing from within. "Pitch me all your ideas."

THANKSGIVING 1943
ONE YEAR LATER

Chapter 17

"All lost children are to be taken up to Twelve," Stella directed the delivery boy who stood before her, wide-eyed, holding the wrist of a thrashing three-year-old who'd lost his parents in an attempt to climb into a delivery truck, wanting to steer it. "Run him up there once they open the doors. Eleanor is up there collecting them all. Trust me, he won't be the only one."

The delivery boy looked panicked. "What will I do with him 'til then?"

Stella dug a gumball out of her coat pocket—a trick she'd learned after last year's reveal.

"Here. That should do it."

"But it's breakfast time."

She winked. "Sometimes you have to break the rules."

Stella brushed the hair from her face and turned back to watch this year's rather windy ribbon cutting. A cold breeze had been whipping down the parade route for the entire procession, and the newspapers had forecasted snow tonight.

The Pittsburgh mayor—a last-minute replacement for Governor Williams who'd just lost his reelection— stepped to the center of the ribbon. "Now, I'd like to officially present Santa Claus with the key to the city.

Mr. Claus, we know your heart and home is in the North Pole. But know that you and Mrs. Claus are always welcome in our city."

With that, the mayor handed over the oversized wooden key to Santa. Mrs. Claus—a new addition this year—stood next to him, offering a matronly nod. Flashbulbs popped as the photographers angled for a few shots.

"Well, on behalf of Mrs. Claus and I, we thank you." Santa bowed his head.

Martin had retired last year. This year's Santa didn't quite live up to Martin's dedication to the role, but what he lacked in professional experience, he made up for in looks—he was plump and his demeanor was grandfatherly, which made him a good fit. Best of all, his wife was more than willing to play Mrs. Claus, which no other store had offered before.

Once the applause subsided, new Santa continued. "Now, my long-time pal on the Nice List, Ira Hanover and I have a gift for the city to enjoy. These beautiful windows behind us!"

This year's theme was *Toys Come to Life!* The series was lined with scenes dedicated to oversized trains, dolls, airplanes, and more—Stella's full concept again. It was a bit more fantastical, offering families an escape from the fact that America was even deeper in the war. She'd hired a professional from Chicago who had no problem being monitored during the installation and felt more than comfortable bringing in a handful of store clerks to help, including Joyce and Mina (who'd moved from Santa Belle to Cosmetics after the holidays). Mina was also now officially going with Billy, who'd enlisted in the Army on his birthday. She'd bring in his letters to read to the new group each time she got one (well, the parts she could read aloud at least).

As Stella stood there waiting for the ribbon to be snipped, it was impossible not to think of the old group from last year who'd thrown so much effort into saving the tradition for the city.

Alfred had moved on to lead the construction of this year's Santa's Village.

John had dropped construction to lead a new wartime project up in the auditorium, helping locals sign up to join the Army.

Luella had gotten sick and moved in with her grown son. Stella had sent her clippings from last year's ribbon-cutting that showed her painting behind Santa. She'd responded with a handwritten thank you note.

Ruth, of course, ran the Luxury Gown department with her reputation still flawless. She'd also been the one who'd introduced her new seamstress, a girl from Sicily, to Gio. Stella wasn't sure if they were going together or not—but Gio had stopped pursuing her almost overnight.

"All right!" Ira shouted over the crowd noise. "What do you say we unwrap these windows, Santa? Mrs. Claus?"

The crowd counted down from three. The ribbon snipped. The crowd cheered.

"Stella? Hey, Stella West!" a voice called from the press riser.

She spotted a reporter pushing his way through the crowd to get to her.

Her eyes widened. "Charlie!"

Charlie was a finance reporter that she'd met through Hector—one Stella had gotten to know rather well over the past year.

She leaned in once he was close enough. "Did you get it for me?"

"Yes. Grabbed it this morning. Forgive me, but I gotta get in there quick." Charlie flipped open his bag and handed her a carefully rolled-up sheet of newspaper tied with a ribbon. "Good luck."

"Thanks." She didn't dare unroll it. She'd just have to trust that Charlie had gotten it perfect.

Hector appeared behind Stella as the curtains drew back.

"Morning, Stells-Bells," he whispered to her.

"Good morning, Hector Donovan."

He looked perfect as usual. Black hair slicked to the side. A gray suit, a black scarf, and a matching fedora with a sprig of holly tucked in the ribbon.

Of course, it wasn't really "good morning." Stella had been spending the night at Hector's apartment semi-regularly since the window unveiling last year. To avoid awkward conversations with her dad, she'd told him she'd started taking on overnight shifts at the store, which his Irish-Catholic mind believed, or at least pretended to.

From their first night together, life with Hector was an adventure.

She'd never thought much of her own figure, except to complain that her chest was too small, or her waist exactly four inches wider than she'd wished, and she'd certainly never had the urge to look at her own backside in the mirror. But to Hector, it was like Rita Hayworth had just walked in the room. Whenever they were alone, his wide hands would explore her until they both were breathless. She was fascinated with all the different ways their bodies could fit together, the feeling of his warm skin on hers, the noises that she could draw out of him.

The low gasp he'd make just before, then the roll of his head back just after.

Not following the rules had its benefits. The entire year, Stella felt like the cat that'd got the canary.

Not that their connection was purely physical. Of course, it wasn't. Looking back on it, she'd loved him long before they'd first kissed last November. Maybe since the first time she'd picked up the telephone that first day in Stuffy McDuffy's etiquette class. Now, they took the trolley into work each day and still spent lunch breaks with one another. On the weekends, they'd do pure and decent courtship things like take walks, go ice skating, have dinner with her dad or occasionally meet him at Mass. (Oh, the confessions that Hector inspired!).

"Whatcha got there?" Hector nodded to the rolled-up newspaper she had tucked under her arm.

"Oh, just something for later."

"For later, huh?" Hector squinted at her, suspicious. He started to back away toward the store as the ribbon was cut and the spectators pushed in. "I'll see you later, right? At four?

"Under the clock. Me and Mr. Snowmin."

When the crowd finally thinned out, Stella carefully slipped the ribbon off the single sheet of newspaper, butterflies filling her tummy. There in big block letters under the *Gazette* banner was the headline that she'd asked Charlie if he could possibly, pretty please, for ten dollars, have printed up for her, on just one sheet of paper, for a special occasion.

When she confided in him what the occasion was, he'd thought she'd gone bats, but he obliged and promised to stay mum.

She took a deep breath, her eyes running over the headline.

Role Reversal: Famed City Publicist Says 'Yes' to Dame's Marriage Proposal!

She almost laughed as she rolled it back up. Charlie wasn't far off. She was bats. Of course, she was. But normal rules never exactly worked for her and Hector.

Stella tucked the paper under her arm—she'd wait until they were both done at four o'clock to give it to him. She headed into the store to start her chaos-filled day of fixing windows and returning lost children.

Even though she'd never heard of a woman proposing, she wasn't nervous to try. Stella knew she would likely botch the words, screw something up—but that was what Hector loved about her.

She was almost certain he'd say yes.

Because engaged or not, Hector already felt like her home.

ACKNOWLEDGMENTS

This piece of historical fiction began as an exercise inspired by dear writing friends, Andrew and Maithy, and snowballed into a Christmas love story dedicated to the city I grew up in. Stella's story brings to life the many memories and holiday traditions that the people of Pittsburgh have enjoyed for generations.

Thank you to my mom for taking me to department stores during the holidays that served as the inspiration for this story, and who listened to me complain about my sore feet after working long holiday shifts.

Thank you to Chad, my husband, for establishing precious Christmastime traditions for our own family.

Special thanks to the newspapers of the city of Pittsburgh, which provided amazing archival inspiration.

9 7 9 8 2 1 8 2 1 3 6 6 4